Kate Bold

Bestselling author Kate Bold is author of the ALEXA CHASE SUSPENSE THRILLER series, comprising six books (and counting); the ASHLEY HOPE SUSPENSE THRILLER series, comprising six books (and counting); the CAMILLE GRACE FBI SUSPENSE THRILLER series, comprising five books (and counting); and the HARLEY COLE FBI SUSPENSE THRILLER series, comprising three books (and counting).

An avid reader and lifelong fan of the mystery and thriller genres, Kate loves to hear from you, so please feel free to visit www.kateboldauthor.com to learn more and stay in touch.

ISBN: 978-1-0943-9544-9

THE KILLING FOG

(An Alexa Chase Suspense Thriller—Book 5)

Kate Bold

BOOKS BY KATE BOLD

ALEXA CHASE SUSPENSE THRILLER
THE KILLING GAME (Book #1)
THE KILLING TIDE (Book #2)
THE KILLING HOUR (Book #3)
THE KILLING POINT (Book #4)
THE KILLING FOG (Book #5)
THE KILLING PLACE (Book #6)

ASHLEY HOPE SUSPENSE THRILLER
LET ME GO (Book #1)
LET ME OUT (Book #2)
LET ME LIVE (Book #3)
LET ME BREATHE (Book #4)
LET ME FORGET (Book #5)
LET ME ESCAPE (Book #6)

CAMILLE GRACE FBI SUSPENSE THRILLER
NOT ME (Book #1)
NOT NOW (Book #2)
NOT WELL (Book #3)
NOT HER (Book #4)
NOT NORMAL (Book #5)

HARLEY COLE FBI SUSPENSE THRILLER
NOWHERE SAFE (Book #1)
NOWHERE LEFT (Book #2)
NOWHERE TO RUN (Book #3)

PROLOGUE

Golden Greens Country Club, Phoenix, Arizona
11:30 PM

Celeste Feinstein was a little drunk, a little irritated, and crushingly bored. Smiling at a passing waiter to indicate she wanted another glass of champagne (her third, Daddy always reminded her to keep count) she nodded as an elderly attorney droned on about some case while never taking his eyes off the low hemline of her red evening dress.

As the attorney made a grandiose gesture to accompany the culmination of what he thought was a gripping courtroom drama with him as the star, looking up at the ceiling in his enthusiasm, Celeste took the chance to glance around the room for a better conversation partner.

The ballroom of the country club was packed with the stars of central Arizona's legal profession. Daddy stood in a circle of gray-haired senior partners, all nodding and hanging on his every word. Other circles of attorneys, ninety percent male, were deep in conversation or debate, their volume dictated by their blood alcohol level. Daddy never raised his voice. He said that if you spoke softly, it made people strain to hear you, subconsciously prompting themselves to increase the importance they gave to your words.

She couldn't practice that with this blowhard. He was so full of himself he wouldn't let her get in a word edgewise. It didn't matter that she had been top of her class at Harvard Law School and at thirty-one was the youngest junior partner in the state. It didn't matter that she refused to take a job in Daddy's firm, wanting to make her own way in the world. It didn't matter that she had just won a big case.

No. Many of these guys—far, far too many—didn't see beyond her blonde hair, attractive body, and youth. They would always talk down or talk about themselves.

Celeste surveyed the sumptuous ballroom with its crystal chandelier, red carpet, and photos of famous golf players, looking for an exit strategy. Join Daddy? No. She'd be in his shadow. Go talk to the folks at Anderson and Cohen? No. A local golf celebrity, invited because he was an instructor at the club, was holding forth on the world's most boring game. Join the younger crowd of junior partners and rising stars? That would have been a good strategy earlier in the evening, before they got tanked.

She decided she didn't need an exit strategy. Celeste waited until the attorney in front of her took a breath, shot him a smile dazzling for him to take his eyes off her breasts for a moment, and said, "Really, George, you've outdone yourself this time. Bravo!"

The older man flushed with pride, or alcohol. Or both. He opened his mouth to continue and Celeste cut him off.

"I'm sorry, but I really must speak with someone for a moment. Upcoming case."

"You sure do work hard, Celeste. You need to cut loose a little," he said in that patronizing way that said she was too driven in her career. As if anyone in this room wasn't driven in their career. Of course, it was all right for men to be driven in their career, but women? They needed to "cut loose a little."

What she needed was some air.

She glided through the crowd, smiling at the important people, nodding to coworkers, raising her glass in a toast to a junior partner of a rival firm who had just scored a courtroom victory. Daddy had told her to always be nice to everyone, because you never knew when you'd need them. Daddy was a darling. While he of course didn't really know what it was like to be a woman in a male-dominated profession, he had always encouraged her and poured his decades of experience into her head. He had done everything he could to set her up for success.

"The rest is up to you," he told her on her graduation day.

And she had done well. Case after victorious case had proven that to everyone. Even the stuffy old men were beginning to show a glimmer of respect.

Just a glimmer, mind you.

She passed through two large glass doors, open to the night, and took in a deep breath of warm evening air.

The club's spacious garden was famous. It took up a whole ten acres of lush lawn, marble fountains, and amusing topiary. The club had imported the same team of expert French landscapers who maintained the gardens at Versailles. They had created what one local magazine called, "A jewel in the desert."

More importantly, at this hour the garden was quiet. Besides a few smokers standing near the door, she saw no one.

Celeste decided to go for a little walk. Not too far. She still had business to do back in that circus, but she needed to clear her head for a minute.

And what a place to clear her head! As she passed between twin rows of bushes sculpted like leaping deer and dancing monkeys, she could almost believe she was in some noble estate in the European countryside, not in the middle of the Southwest's biggest city. Only the glow of Phoenix all around her obscuring the stars overhead reminded her of the more than a million and a half people around her. That and the bush sculpted to look like a golfer teeing up. You won't find one of those in Versailles.

Sometimes she wished she could spend more time in the country. For a rising attorney, however, this city was the place to be. And once she had established herself, she still wouldn't be able to leave. Celeste knew she'd have to remain satisfied with the family retreat in the pine forest near Flagstaff, and occasional trips to rural Italy and France.

Still, it wasn't a bad life …

"Couldn't stand that party either, eh?"

Celeste jumped enough that some of her champagne sloshed out of her glass to splash on her wrist.

"Oh, sorry for startling you. I thought you saw me."

A handsome man holding a champagne glass stepped out from a side path that led to the koi pond.

"It's all right," Celeste said, trying to slow down her heart.

Another look at him set it racing again.

He was an athletic man with a square jaw and blonde buzzcut. He looked about her age, his muscular body nicely filling out his suit.

The suit, she noticed with an expert eye even in this dim light, wasn't as expensive as it should be for this party. But he walked with an erect, confident gait that would make him fit right in.

"I don't believe I've had the pleasure," he said, extending a hand. "Brent Richter."

"Celeste Feinstein." His grip was firm, but didn't linger like some of the letches in there.

"Who do you work for?" Brent asked.

"I'm junior partner at Taylor and Hatchfield," Celeste said, slightly annoyed that he hadn't heard of her. "And you?"

"I just moved here. I'm setting up a private practice. Contract law."

"Good for you. Contract law is booming these days. With the economic downturn, lots of people are trying to weasel their way out of contracts."

"That's what I'm banking on," Brent said. He grinned, showing white, even teeth. He nodded toward the building, where the faint buzz of conversation could be heard. "I got a bit tired of the chatter, though."

"Ugh. I hate these things."

"Necessary for the job. I wish it wasn't. Why can't society let people be who they are?"

Good point, Celeste thought, warming up to him. "I don't think it's much different in any other profession. Come on, let's go look at the koi pond. They leave it lit at night."

They strolled down the path to a large, artificial pond with irregular sides of stone and ferns. A dim light illuminated the water from below as countless large koi swam around, their red and white patterned scales making a hypnotic tapestry.

"Wow!" Brent said. "This is amazing. Thanks for showing me this."

"Didn't you just come this way?"

"Oh, yes. I didn't look in, though. Had my head in the clouds. But about what you were saying before, you're right. It isn't any different in other professions. It's a societal problem. You see, for a society to function, you need to establish certain rules to constrict behavior. Some amount of individual freedom must be sacrificed in the quest for the greater good."

Celeste laughed. "Brent, I'm an attorney. I know this."

Brent nodded. "Of course. But what people don't see is that move actually hurts society. The best members of humanity live on its fringes. It's only there that you find true genius."

Celeste chuckled. "I do criminal law, and I have to say most of my clients don't quite fall in the genius category."

"That's a sampling error. You're only dealing with people who have been caught."

Celeste took a sip, still staring at the lovely fish. "I suppose you have a point there."

"Not only *a* point, but *the* point," Brent said, obviously warming to his subject. "Society is led from its fringes. Looks at the tech billionaires. All geeks no one paid any attention to in high school.

Bullied and no girlfriends. Now they're running the world. And the fringe painters and sculptors who started new artistic movements, laughed at in their time and now known the world over. Then there are those who made a mark through violence. Genghis Khan and Tamerlane. Lizzie Borden and Jack the Ripper."

"You have some interesting choices there," Celeste said. *Talking about geeks ...*

Celeste, already thinking of exit strategies, glanced at her odd companion. The light from the koi pond lit him from beneath, casting dark shadows around his jaw and eyes. It shone brightest on his shoes and trousers, and Celeste noted with surprise his leather dress shoes were dirty and scuffed, and there was a small tear on his left trouser leg.

"You get in a fight with a cactus?" Celeste said, pointing.

"Oh, that? No, that came from climbing the fence. It was taller than I thought, and when I got over I landed in a flower bed."

"What?"

Brent turned to her. "You see, for a man to really be free, he has to ignore society's rules, strike out on his own. Only then can he move society forward through his shining example."

"You climbed the fence?"

"And society needs such shining examples, today more than ever."

Celeste stepped away back to the path leading back to the resort building. "That's very interesting, but they'll be expecting me back. Work. You know how it is."

"Oh, but Celeste, at least let me give you my calling card."

"Sure." *Straight into the recycle bin with that one, weirdo.*

Brent reached into the inside pocket of his suit and pulled out a strange object. It was a wooden and metal handle a little longer than his hand. Celeste blinked, and stared.

Only when he pressed a button on the side and a small blade flicked out did she realize it was a switchblade.

"I like to go old school," Brent said, rushing for her.

Celeste had just enough time to scream, although her scream got drowned out by a burst of laughter coming from the resort building. Daddy had probably told another of his famous jokes.

Brent's hand clamped on her mouth and Celeste felt the hot pain of the blade piercing her abdomen.

She dropped her champagne glass, which fell soundlessly on the grass, and struggled as the blade pierced her body again and again.

So quick, he was stabbing her so quickly, his reddened face twisted with glee as her knees buckled and he knelt by her as she lay prone. The world began to fade, the pain became distant, but still he stabbed that little blade into her.

Again and again and again.

CHAPTER ONE

U.S. Deputy Marshal Alexa Chase drove down the darkened desert road, hands slick on the steering wheel, peering into the desert on either side as far as her high beams would penetrate, every now and then shouting out the open window.

"Stacy!"

When she wasn't calling out her thirteen-year-old neighbor's name, she was steadily, loudly, relentlessly cursing.

Alexa knew she was acting crazy, but how else could she act? Stacy had finally done it. She had threatened to for more than a year now, and she had finally done it. She had finally run away from home.

Stomach sick with worry, Alexa checked her phone, as she had every two minutes since Stacy had been reported missing. The search party her partner Stuart Barrett had organized sent in regular updates from the places they had been posted—the bus stations and movie theaters, the highways in and out of nearby Phoenix, and the red light districts in that sprawling city.

Alexa shuddered to think what could happen to a thirteen-year-old girl on the streets of Phoenix.

Assuming that's where she went. While it was the most obvious destination, and the most familiar to her, that didn't mean the kid had headed that direction. She could have hopped a bus or hitched a ride somewhere else.

That's why Alexa was scouring the roads around Stacy's trailer in the rural area north of Phoenix. Maybe she'd come across the kid thumbing a ride.

Or come across her tossed to the side of the road after having been taken for a ride.

Tears welled up in her eyes. Alexa quickly wiped them away so she could see the road. She had been in law enforcement too long. She knew the dangers out there all too well. Her mind filled with a thousand terrible scenarios.

"Where the hell is that kid?"

Guilt washed over her. This was all her fault.

Alexa came to an intersection, a crossing of two rural roads stretching into the dark desert night. She hit the brakes on her Jeep, tires squealing, and stopped right in the middle.

She had no idea where to go.

Alexa grabbed her phone and called Stacy's father.

The phone rang, and rang.

"Come on, already!"

Mr. Carpenter picked up.

"Yeah?" he grunted.

"Is she back?" Alexa asked.

"What? Oh, you mean Stacy?"

Alexa resisted the urge to smash the phone against her dashboard. Her neighbor sounded drunk as usual. No wonder Stacy wanted to run away.

"Yes, I mean Stacy," she managed to say without swearing.

"Did you check Billy's house?"

Billy was a senior at her school, seventeen years old and caught trying to sneak out at night with Stacy. The blowup that caused made Alexa punish her for the frist time since they'd met. She'd told the girl that she could no longer come over to the ranch anytime she wanted.

That had been the final straw for the kid. Alexa, in a fit of anger, had taken away Stacy's only safe space.

Stupid, I was so stupid.

"Yes. As I told you, we checked on him and his parents are on the watch for her. The parents are decent people and will inform us if she turns up."

"If the parents were decent people, their son wouldn't be catting around with a girl four years younger."

Alexa curled her lip in disgust. Like he and his useless wife had a right to criticize other people's parenting!

"Can you think of any place she might have gone?" She had asked him this before and he had only said the obvious places Stuart had already checked.

"No."

"Have you been checking the desert around your trailer?" Alexa asked, peering in all four directions from the center of the intersection. Some headlights approached from the left. Alexa put her Jeep in reverse to get out of the way.

"I told you, she's just gone off to let off some steam. She'll be back in a few hours. I used to do that all the time when I argued with my dad."

Yeah, and look how you turned out.

"It's very dangerous for her to be out this late at night, Mr. Carpenter. Please continue calling all her friends and your neighbors."

"I will."

Alexa wasn't convinced.

The vehicle passed the intersection in front of her. Her high beams illuminated a windowless van. In the front cab she caught a glimpse of a heavyset man and a blonde girl with a ponytail.

Just like Stacy.

CHAPTER TWO

Alexa tossed her phone on the seat next to her and hit the gas. She screeched around the hard turn and barreled down the rural highway after them. The van's rear lights drew closer and closer as Alexa accelerated. There were no windows on the back of the van, either.

It was one of those vehicles the schoolkids called a "pedo van."

As she came up behind, Alexa hit a button and the magnetic police light she had affixed to her roof when she had set out began to flash, the siren wailing across the desert like the mystical La Llorona.

An old Mexican legend. The ghost of a young mother who had lost her children and wandered the night, crying for them for all eternity.

The van put on its indicator and pulled off to the side of the road. Alexa hit the brakes and cut in front of it, blocking it at an angle.

Pulling out her gun and a flashlight, she hopped out of her Jeep and pointed both at the front seat.

"Get out of the vehicle! You're … "

Her voice trailed off and she saw the stunned faces of the driver and her passenger. The girl in the passenger's seat wasn't a girl at all, just a petite woman with the lines of middle age who wore her blonde hair in a ponytail like Stacy.

"Oh my God. Sorry."

Before the stunned civilians could say anything, Alexa hopped back in the Jeep and drove away. She couldn't waste any more time.

She continued her search, peering into the desert and calling out Stacy's name. Updates from the search party revealed no one had seen her or heard anything about her from people Stacy knew. Word had spread, and Stuart had added several people to the chat group. Off-duty colleagues. Parents of Stacy's friends. Teachers. A nightshift taxi driver Stuart played pool with. He was roping in anyone who had any chance of hearing from her or spotting her on the streets.

Bless that man. He's going all out for us. And he knows I'm too damn frantic to organize it myself.

Where the hell did she go? It's like she headed into the desert and vanished.

Alexa drove along, her worried mind running through a dozen of the most terrible scenarios every second, while her unconscious began to make a string of associations, dimly heard beneath the grinding anxiety.

Vanished in the desert. Expert at hiding. The law can't find her. Girl hiding from the police. Vanished in the desert. Apache warriors hiding in the desert from the U.S. Cavalry. Apache families hiding out too.

Apache families ...

Apache women ...

The old Apache woman!

Alexa hit the brakes and did a 180 so quickly she nearly flipped the Jeep.

In the countryside a couple of miles north of Alexa's ranch and Stacy's neighboring trailer was a box canyon with a steep cliff at the end. The weathered stone had taken on a vague resemblance to an old Native American woman, especially in the moonlight.

Like tonight.

It was one of Stacy's favorite spots to ride to on nights of the full moon, when the desert was turned into a serene, silvery landscape that was as surreal as it was beautiful. They had gone there several times, Alexa recounting stories of the Apaches and the famous warrior woman Lozen, who fought alongside the men back in the nineteenth century to keep her people free.

Alexa had explained that box canyons like this one were a favorite place for the Apaches to hide. The U.S. Cavalry thought they could seal off the end of the canyon and trap them inside. But the Apaches, experts at climbing, could always get out the supposedly dead end, while their warriors lined both clifftops, raining arrows on the troops as they charged into the canyon. It would be a trap, all right, but for the soldiers, not the Apaches.

"Wow, so this was the safest place in the desert for them," Alexa recalled Stacy saying one night.

The safest place in the desert. A good place to hide. Familiar and not far from home.

Alexa had been so worried that Stacy would act like a regular runaway, she had forgotten how in love she was with the desert and all its ways. It was one of the things they bonded over.

Despite being a member of law enforcement, Alexa drove at ninety back to her ranch, blowing every red light and stop sign she came to.

She stopped in her dirt driveway in a plume of dust, leapt out, and hurried to the stable behind her house where she kept Smith and Wesson, her two horses.

As she flicked on the light in the wooden building, she saw the two horses in their stalls, curried and munching contentedly on some oats.

Alexa felt a lump in her throat. She had told Stacy that as punishment for planning to sneak into her house to do God-knows-what with her inappropriately old boyfriend, she was no longer allowed to come over and feed them.

The girl had defied her, sneaking in to say goodbye to two of the most reliable friends she had in the world.

She saddled up Wesson, led him out of the stable and to the north trail, mounted, and rode off into the night.

Usually when she and Stacy went to the box canyon, they went on a full moon. Right now it was only a waxing half, and so the way was dimmer than Alexa was accustomed to. And yet she didn't want to use her flashlight. It would warn Stacy that she was coming, assuming she was even there, and the girl might do something stupid.

Alexa had made it a mile, the lights of her ranch and the Carpenter trailer fading behind her, before she realized she hadn't even thought of notifying her parents.

After all, why should she?

Alexa shook her head in disgust. Those two worked when they felt like it, got as much social services as they could scam, and drank every night and almost every day. No wonder their kid didn't want to live there!

It had been like this ever since the Carpenters had bought the old trailer near her house and moved in two years ago. She had first noticed Stacy, back then an effusive little girl instead of an eye-rolling teen, the very first day. As her parents unloaded boxes and a few junky pieces of furniture from a beat-up old pickup, she had stood in the stretch of open land between their properties, staring at Smith and Wesson.

She stood out there staring the next day too. Closer this time.

On the third day, Alexa went over to introduce herself. She wore her U.S. Marshals uniform because she was due to head out for a shift.

The reaction from the two adults told her a lot.

“We don’t know nothing about it!” Mr. Carpenter shouted before she made it hallway to their trailer.

“Nothing about what?” she asked, still approaching.

Mrs. Carpenter appeared beside him, an overweight, tired-looking woman with a nose to rival Rudolph the Red-Nosed Reindeer’s.

“Whatever it is you come to ask about,” she said.

“I’m your neighbor,” Alexa explained. “I just came over to say hi.”

That relaxed them a bit. In the polite but strained conversation that followed, Alexa learned three things.

One, they were both mildly inebriated even though it was ten in the morning.

Two, they didn’t seem to be on the run from the law, just routinely worried about getting into trouble. That fit in with observation number one. When Alexa checked later, she didn’t find anything worse than three DUIs and one drunk and disorderly.

Three, and this was the biggest observation, was that their daughter was an intelligent girl who really, really needed a friend.

This got proven when she bounded out of the trailer with a big hello and ten thousand questions about the horses. Alexa tried to answer each question before Stacy asked the next one, amused at how enthusiastic this kid was. She had never been riding, Stacy told her, but loved horses.

Then Alexa made an off-the-cuff remark that changed both of their lives.

“You’ll have to come over and meet them sometime.”

This made Stacy leap in the air and ask her parents if she could go over, “Right now. Pleasepleasepleasepleaseplease?”

Her parents replied with a shrug.

“Do what you want, girl,” the mom said. “Just remember I’m cooking up mac and cheese at six, and if you ain’t here, you don’t eat.”

Alexa couldn’t believe it. They had been acquainted for all of ten minutes and they were leaving their child with her? Sure, she was a woman and in uniform, but still.

So Alexa called the office to say she’d be an hour late, and gave Stacy her first ride. She was over at the ranch nearly every day after that. The kid was a natural in the saddle, and desperate for the approval her ability earned her.

And Alexa found herself desperate for company. She had discovered that busting bad guys (and busting a few heads in the process) wasn't the only way to gain satisfaction in life. Sure, she had her own family, a small but loyal circle of friends, and her horses, but her career took up so much of her time and energy it felt good to enjoy some simple good times with a happy kid.

A happy kid? Yes, when she was with the horses and things weren't too bad at home.

At least Alexa had thought so. Now she knew a lot more had bubbled beneath the surface.

While most of the blame lay on her useless parents, Alexa had to admit she wasn't entirely innocent. Stacy needed a role model, a companion. Someone to be there for her. But Alexa was always rushing off on the next case, never knowing when she'd be back home.

Stacy put a brave face on it and took care of the horses. Deep down, Alexa now knew, the girl had felt abandoned. Over and over again. Another adult had disappointed her.

I'll fix this, Alexa promised herself. *Just let her be all right and I'll fix this.*

Alexa could see the rocky ridge up ahead, a dark bulk against the starry sky. She perked her ears and strained her eyes, searching with expert senses honed from years of desert living and policework for any sign of her.

Strange how often I've done this with escaped prisoners or criminals on the run, she thought. *Never done this with a teenager before.*

Well, there was that eighteen-year-old meth dealer wanted for stabbing his own father, but he doesn't count.

She heard and saw nothing except for the distant lonesome call of a coyote. Alexa urged Wesson along the familiar landscape until she saw a dent in the top of the cliff's silhouette signaling the entrance to the box canyon. The ground sloped down, the cliff loomed closer, and she began to see it as stone instead of shadow, with a darker space, barely wide enough for a woman and a girl to ride side by side, running into the ridge.

She entered the box canyon.

Moonlight cast an eerie glow on the rock wall to her right. The moon had not yet risen high enough to illuminate the canyon floor or the wall to her left, so she slowed Wesson and picked along the rough terrain with care. The canyon turned slightly, and as she rounded the bend she saw the back of the canyon.

A flashlight winked out. Alexa's heart leapt.

"It's me!" Alexa called out.

Please be alone.

"Go away!" Stacy's voice cried back.

Alexa felt so relieved she almost fell of her horse. Her muscles, drawn as tight as violin strings, eased. Then another worry tensed them again.

"Are you alone?"

"Yeah, and I want to be."

Her voice sounded scared, uncertain. Alexa kept riding toward the back of the canyon.

Although the moon cast no light on the ground, Alexa's dark-adapted eyes could discern a rough camp, complete with a sleeping bag, a couple of white plastic supermarket bags that probably held food plundered from her parents' understocked kitchenette, and a few other things scattered around that she couldn't make out.

She also saw Stacy, standing near the back of the canyon.

"You all right?" Alexa asked, dismounting and tethering Wesson to a big rock near Stacy's campsite.

Her question was greeted with silence.

Alexa walked over to her.

"Leave me alone," Stacy said, crossing her arms over her chest. "Don't you have some case to run off to?"

"No."

At least not at the moment.

Alexa gave her a hug. Stacy stood stiff and still, unresponsive.

"You been out here the whole time?" Alexa asked.

"What do you care?"

Alexa kept hugging her, then turned her gently to face the back wall of the box canyon. The moon cast slanting rays down on the rough rock wall, and the pattern of light and shadow created the semblance of a wide-faced woman, her features lined with concern and determination.

"Lozen looks even better under a half moon," Alexa said.

"Less light to see by. That makes it better to sneak around the soldiers."

Alexa nudged her. "And sneak around annoying parents."

"Big time." The words sounded bitter, but the agreement, the conspiracy to defy that useless pair, softened them somewhat.

Alexa didn't like to criticize Stacy's parents, but she was desperate to break the ice. And perhaps not talking about the problem, always skirting around it, had stopped any real solution.

"I bet Lozen kicked some guys' asses in those days," Alexa said.

Stacy laughed, her muscles easing. "Totally."

Then she stiffened up again, remembering she was supposed to be angry.

"Thanks for feeding Smith and Wesson," Alexa said.

"Well, it was the last time I'm going to see them," Stacy snapped.

"You're seeing Wesson right now."

That made them both turn, just in time to see Wesson drop a pile a manure on Stacy's sleeping bag.

"Oh my God, that's so gross!"

"You've shoveled heaps of the stuff."

"Yeah, but I never had it land where I sleep."

They both laughed. Alexa hugged her a little tighter.

"Well, there's no horse manure in your room. Come on. You got school tomorrow."

Stacy clicked her tongue. "School is boring."

"I'll drive you in. That way you'll have time to take a short ride in the morning."

"I'm not going back there. Ever."

"You have to," Alexa said gently.

Stacy pulled away. "School is boring, and I can't even date the boys I want to date, and my parents are a pain in the ass, and I can't even come over to the ranch anytime I want to anymore."

Alexa hugged her again, stroking her blonde hair. "I'm sorry. That was wrong of me. I know how important it is to you to come over."

"You don't know what it's like living with them!" she said, her voice cracking.

Alexa squeezed her tighter. The kid was right, she didn't know what it was like to live with two drunkass, useless parents. While her own father had always been a bit gruff and distant, something that had grown worse when her mother had died when she was younger than Stacy was now, Alexa had known she would be cared for. She had known she was loved, too, even though her dad wasn't capable of showing it.

"I'm sorry to take the ranch away. You can come over anytime you want. You're like family to me, Stacy. And sometimes family gets mad at each other. It doesn't mean we care any less. Real family gets over that sort of thing."

"I wouldn't know," Stacy grumbled.

No, I guess you wouldn't.

Alexa pulled away a little and lifted up the girl's chin to make her look at her.

"Now you do."

Pause.

"Am I in trouble?"

"No, but you've caused a lot of trouble. You had us worried sick."

"You. Not them."

Alexa knew Stacy meant her parents. She opened her mouth to object, but the lie caught in her throat.

Stacy was right. They hadn't been worried.

"Don't do it again. I've told you what happens to runaways and I couldn't stand that happening to you."

"I can take care of myself."

"Come on, let's gather up your stuff."

"And then what? Back to the trailer and you running off on some case?"

Alexa paused. What to say?

"Yes. I know you hate the trailer, but one day you'll be old enough to live on your own and you can put it all behind you. And yes, I'll have another case soon, but I always come home, don't I? I promise that no matter what, I'll be there at night for you."

"Promise?"

"Promise."

They gathered up Stacy's things in silence, shaking off the sleeping bag as well as they could and stuffing it into one of the supermarket bags. The stone face looked down at them in silence. Alexa remembered something her mother, now long dead, had once told her.

Never make a promise you can't keep.

Because Alexa had a meeting with Drake Logan tomorrow. She needed some answers from him. But talking to that guy was sure to stress her out and mess with her head, and she needed to keep her head clear to take care of Stacy. If she snapped at the kid, or seemed distant, Stacy might take that as rejection.

And that could prove to be the breaking point.

CHAPTER THREE

Special Agent Stuart Barrett of the FBI picked up his phone, his eyes still scanning the Greyhound station in downtown Phoenix, looking for a young, blonde girl in the waiting room or boarding one of the buses that rumbled through the glaringly lit parking lot.

"I found her!"

Alexa's voice, which had sounded past the edge of panic on her half-hourly progress calls to him, now carried the note of hysterical relief.

"Is she OK?" Stuart asked.

"Yes, thank God. She's fine. Totally fine." Stuart could hear her suppress a sob on the other end of the line.

Stuart closed his eyes and let out a long, slow breath of relief. Until that moment he hadn't realized how wound up he had been ever since his partner had made the panicked call that tore him out of bed and calling in favors with everybody he knew in town to help with the search.

He had lost someone named Stacy once. His high school girlfriend who had been abducted and never found. That loss had cast a shadow over the following years he could never escape.

His old girlfriend and Alexa's neighbor weren't much alike. That didn't matter. The name was enough.

Alexa's voice snapped him out of it. "You still there?"

It sounded like she had asked that already.

"Yeah. Sorry. You take care. And tell her she nearly gave me a fricking heart attack."

Alexa laughed, far too loudly.

"I'll talk to you soon," she said, and hung up.

Stuart shook his head as he sent a message to the group text of searchers. Stacy was a good kid but a heap of trouble, most of that trouble caused by her useless parents. While he admired Alexa for taking the girl under her wing, he worried about the toll it took on her.

Tonight, it had taken a toll on him too. He had been concerned about Stacy ever since meeting her a couple of months before, but in a second-hand sort of way, knowing that Alexa was doing as good of a job as she could. Stacy was lucky to have her.

But tonight, when she had run away from home, his gut had twisted, his pulse had raced, and he had tirelessly organized a search party.

Now his gut began to unknot itself. Slowly. He needed a back rub. Maybe a front rub too. Or one of those hot oil massages. His girlfriend, Anette Guevara, was a genius at more than just Crime Scene Investigation. She was a genius at all things erotic.

He sent her a text. "Hey beautiful. We found her. Can I come over?"

Stuart strolled over to his car and headed out. His phone kept pinging and he kept checking it to find search party members texting him back to say how happy they were. One retired cop, a friend of a friend who neither Stuart nor Alexa actually knew, had volunteered to scour the truck stops. He suggested some celebratory beers. Stuart's phone started pinging like crazy after that.

He set his phone on the passenger's seat as he drove, letting it ping. He'd never see Annette's message under the stream of dialog going on in his phone right now. It didn't matter. Stuart knew the answer. If she wasn't picking over dead bodies, she was always happy to see him.

Humming to himself, he sped through downtown Phoenix to her apartment. Annette had a nice little one-bedroom place with a balcony overlooking the apartment complex's pool and jacuzzi. They'd had a lot of fun in those late at night. Annette had a kink for the outdoors. She had a kink for a lot of things.

Imagine, an apartment complex with a pool and a Jacuzzi that didn't charge exorbitant rates! In fact, most apartment complexes here seemed to have them. So different than back East. He was beginning to like Arizona.

Taking the streets at a safe twenty miles an hour over the speed limit, Stuart made it to Annette's place in only a quarter of an hour. Briefly he wondered if he should grab some wine on the way, then decided against it. She had work the next day. As crazy and as fun as his girlfriend could be, she was as devoted to catching the bad guys as he or his partner Alexa were.

So no wine, but maybe the Jacuzzi. Or maybe one of those stand-up massages they gave each other while standing in a piping hot shower. They always enjoyed those.

Or maybe something else. Annette could be amazingly creative.

He parked, then checked himself in the rearview mirror, patting down some windblown hair and blowing into his cupped hand to make sure his breath smelled all right. Finding himself presentable, he hopped out and, whistling a happy tune, hurried up the outside stairs to her apartment.

Stuart felt a warm tingle as he knocked. He loved coming here. While his mind had only been on one thing the whole drive over, he appreciated a lot more than that about Annette. She was funny as hell, a brilliant conversationalist, and if work had worn them both out, they'd often just snuggle up for movie night.

She was brilliant too. A certified genius with a Ph.D. in biology, several commendations from the city, and her peers called her the best crime scene investigator in the entire state. Annette had taught him a lot about criminal investigation and the local underworld.

She had also taught him a lot about Mexican culture and hiking in the desert, two things he'd never explored before coming to the Southwest. He could see why Alexa lived away from the city. There was a subtle beauty to the land here that got under your skin.

If this new collaboration between the FBI and the U.S. Marshals Service became permanent, maybe he'd get a little place in the desert too. A bit of that natural beauty for himself.

Speaking of natural beauties, Stuart could hear Annette moving around in there. His smile broadened. The peephole darkened for a moment, and then Annette opened the door.

Annette Guevara was a petite Mexican-American who looked ten years younger than her thirty-two. That had made Stuart a bit uncomfortable at first, but he had soon gotten over it. He loved her long brown hair, oval face, and liquid brown eyes. He loved her crazy, brilliant personality. He loved pretty much everything about her.

"Oh, I'm so glad she's OK," she said without preamble.

"Yeah, I guess you can tell because I'm here, right?"

"Sure. And you didn't get my text because you had to organize the search party. Alexa would have been too frantic to do it herself. You sent out a message when Stacy got found, then sent me a message asking to come over, and that got buried in all the responses about Stacy."

Stuart laughed. "You're batting a thousand."

Annette didn't laugh along with him. Stuart realized he hadn't even been let into the apartment.

"What's wrong, baby?"

"I wish you had seen my reply," she said with a long face. "I asked you not to come over."

"What's the matter? You sick?"

Annette paused, not meeting his gaze, then heaved out a sigh.

"Come on in."

"What's the matter?"

He entered the apartment and they sat together on the couch. Stuart put an arm around her. When she didn't ease into a hug as usual, he withdrew it.

Annette looked him in the eye and said, "I don't think we should see each other anymore."

"What! Why?"

"I just don't see this going in the right direction."

"The right direction? We get on great."

Annette made a weak little smile and took his hand. "We do, but we want different things. I just want something light, to have fun. You're after something more serious. I don't blame you for that, but I can tell you want to make this a long-term thing and that's not what I'm looking for right now."

"Was it something I did?"

Annette squeezed his hand. "No. You're wonderful. Too wonderful. You want to settle down."

"Wait. I never said anything about settling down. We've only been dating for two months."

"You don't have to say anything. I can tell. Complimenting how I decorate my place. Buying those matching coffee mugs. Suggesting that vacation. You want to get all domestic."

"What's wrong with getting domestic?"

"Nothing. For you. Me? I'm not ready for that. And if I keep going out with you you're going to want it more and more and it will make the inevitable breakup even harder."

"Inevitable breakup? But we get along so great."

"Don't you see? That's the problem!"

"I thought only guys were supposed to have a fear of commitment."

"Har har. I don't have a fear of commitment. I just don't want it at this phase of my life."

Stuart paused, then asked the question he knew he shouldn't.

"Is there someone else?"

Annette groaned. "Ugh! Why do guys always ask that? No, there's no one else. And before you ask, it's not because I feel like dating women now instead of men."

"I never said that."

Annette smiled and squeezed his hand again.

"I know. That was unfair. You're the only guy I ever dated who didn't either get neurotic about my bisexuality or suggested bringing another girl into bed. Thanks for that."

"I can't believe you want to break up with me because we're doing so well."

"I'm sorry. You deserve better. We just want different things."

She stood, letting go of his hand. Stuart could tell that was a signal to leave.

His mind raced. What could he saw to get her to reconsider? He needed the right words!

Then he realized there weren't any right words. She had made up her mind. And now, looking back, she had seemed a little withdrawn for the past week. Stuart had assumed it was the heavy workload. Now he knew better.

Reluctantly, he stood up.

"We're so good together." His objection came out whiney, and made him ashamed.

Annette put a hand on his cheek. "We were. I'm sorry."

She walked to the door and opened it.

She gave him a long, lingering kiss. A goodbye kiss.

A last kiss.

Stuart stepped out the door.

"Oh my God!" Annette cried. "You didn't even suggest one last night. You're too perfect."

She grabbed him by the ears, pulled him in for another kiss, and pushed him away.

"Now get out of here before I make a mistake. I'm sorry."

She slammed the door, leaving Stuart standing there, utterly confused.

He went down the stairs like a sleepwalker, emotions numb.

As he got to the car, it hit him all at once.

He'd lost the best girl he'd had since high school! The best girl since …

… the one who disappeared.

Stuart staggered, both from the breakup that just blindsided him and that terrible loss all those years ago. For a long minute he leaned against his car, unable to do more than breathe.

At last, he got in the car and drove off, his mind swirling with emotions. While he knew he shouldn't, he couldn't help but mingle those two losses.

Stuart had done that before in breakups. It seemed every time he got disappointed romantically, even if he was the one leaving, he'd equate it in his mind with the abduction of his high school sweetheart.

A terrible thing to do. Disrespectful to Stacy's memory and unfair to whoever he was dating at the moment.

He parked in front of a convenience store, too distracted to drive. Stuart sat there for a long time, trying to sort out his thoughts and emotions and achieving nothing except getting more wound up.

I should talk to someone. Get it off my chest.

But who?

In the few months Stuart had been here, he'd been run so ragged by the caseload, and run ragged in a much better way by Annette, he hadn't had time to make any friends. Sure, he had a few guys he shot pool with at his local bar, but they weren't real friends. And he didn't want to bother his aged parents about something like this. They talked too much about how he "needed to stop picking the wrong women and settle down." Stuart wasn't in the mood for that lecture right now.

His older brother? His little brother?

No and no. They'd listen, of course, but they knew nothing about Annette so they wouldn't have any good advice.

Good advice for what? It's not like you're getting back with her.

Still, it would be nice to talk to someone who knows her.

Alexa.

He called, not sure what he would say. He just wanted to speak and have someone listen.

The phone rang and kept on ringing.

Stuart groaned. Of course. Of course she wasn't picking up. She was spending time with Stacy. Her Stacy.

He didn't have a Stacy. Or an Annette. Or anyone this side of the Mississippi.

Stuart sat for a long time in the parking lot, watching people come and go, feeling very much alone.

CHAPTER FOUR

Arizona State Maximum Security Prison, Phoenix
The next day

Alexa took a deep breath and entered the cellblock, flanked by a pair of immense prison guards. They walked abreast through the bowels of the prison, at the far end of one cell block past countless barred gates, alarms, and security cameras. Only the worst of the worst were kept here. As she passed the cells, she recognized several of the glowering inmates featured on Arizona's Most Wanted list from years past.

They wouldn't get on that list again. Everyone was in here for life. No one had ever escaped.

Alexa recognized sexual predators, cold-blooded killers, gang leaders, and human traffickers. She even recognized a one-legged former hitman who had to have his leg amputated after her former partner, U.S. Marshal Robert Powers, blew it off with a 12-gauge shotgun.

He glowered even worse than the others. Alexa smiled back at him as she passed.

Usually when you passed through a cell block the prisoners would bang on their bars, hurl insults and threats, make crude propositions.

None of them did that. They only stood or sat in silence.

The silence made it worse.

The security camera picked up their approach to the final gate and someone in the control room buzzed them through.

That brought them to the final hallway where, right at the end, resided the prison's most dangerous and notorious inmate.

Drake Logan.

Alexa noted that all the other cells on this short hallway were empty. She didn't need to ask why. Logan had a magnetic charisma, one that could bend lesser minds to its will. If he was within earshot of a group of hardened criminals, he'd have an organized gang within days, and its power would reach beyond the prison walls to every relative, friend, and former accomplice those inmates could get in contact with. It had happened before.

And that charisma, that disease of darkness for which Drake Logan was a carrier, that was why Alexa wanted to speak with him.

A red plastic chair had been set in the hallway facing the cell, well out of reach from the bars. It wouldn't have made any difference if he had managed to grab it. Prison issue chairs were of such flimsy material it could barely hold an adult's weight, let alone be turned into a weapon.

Although if anyone could find a way, it would be Drake Logan.

The two guards stopped a little short of the cell, out of sight of its occupant, Alexa noticed.

"We're here if you need us," one said in a low voice.

A mocking bark of laughter came from the cell. "She doesn't need you. She's doesn't need anyone. Alexa is one of the strong. Now go scuttle off and beat some poor bastard who mouthed off to you. The grownups want to talk."

The two guards frowned at the unseen prisoner, but did not reply.

Alexa turned to them. "We'll be all right alone."

The prison guards hesitated, then moved away. Alexa squared her shoulders and walked the rest of the way down the hall.

Drake Logan sat on his prison bunk in the bare cell that would be his home for the rest of his life, a life that would almost certainly end with his last appeal getting rejected and him strapped to a bed getting a lethal injection.

Someone who didn't have eyes to see would not think of this man as a threat. Logan had a small, wiry frame, standing barely five foot eight inches. His soft brown eyes spoke of intelligence and usually looked out on the world with an amused detachment. Someone who didn't have eyes to see would think he was in prison for tax fraud or counterfeiting.

But Alexa did have eyes to see. Even if she didn't know this man's history, she'd know he was dangerous. The way he sat, body coiled and ready to spring even though no one was within reach. It was his natural posture. He probably didn't even know he was doing it.

And then those eyes, which every now and then flashed rage or bottomless contempt. Those eyes always roved, looking for opportunities, or settled on some object of interest with laser-like focus.

At the moment, that meant Alexa.

She sat, the plastic chair bending slightly under her weight.

"You've got a new look," she said.

He had shaved off his normal stubble and shock of unruly brown hair and was now completely hairless except for his eyebrows. Now that the bangs weren't hiding them, she noticed those eyebrows arched to a point in the middle, making him look demonic.

"Got to change it up. Keep them guessing."

"The only thing people around here are guessing about is your date of execution."

Logan smiled, that "I know something you don't" smile that had always irritated her, and put a hand to his thin lips as if to smoke a cigarette, an odd habit of his.

"So to what do I owe the honor?" Logan asked.

Alexa tried to speak, and found she couldn't broach the subject. Instead she made a show of looking around.

"Where are your neighbors?"

"This is death row. I guess they fried them all."

"Lethal injection. Arizona doesn't fry anyone anymore. They might make an exception for you, though."

Logan didn't seem phased by this taunt, merely annoyed.

"Cut to the chase, Alexa. You're here on a visit, almost certainly without your boss's knowledge. You didn't come all this way to tease me like we were in middle school."

"I'm not teasing you. I'm merely enjoying the thought of you getting executed. I've reserved a front row seat."

Logan smiled. "Aw, come on, Alexa. You know you don't mean that. You love having me around."

"No, I hate having you around."

"You hate that you love it. Come on. Tell me what's on your mind. You have no one else to talk to. No one who understands. No fellow hunter like me."

Alexa paused, feeling backed into a corner. She had questions that she needed answered, but she'd rather ask anyone than this smug psychopath sitting behind bars and somehow having all the power.

She'd rather be anywhere but here, with anyone but him.

But ever since reading Robert Powers's journal, which he had specifically left her in his will, she had been struggling with the revelation that Logan and the man who had originally hunted him down had hung out in high school. Even worse, Powers had looked up to him.

We all looked up to him. The cool older guy who bought us beer and could get us weed, even though I never wanted that. Some kids thought it was cool that he had dropped out. I never understood why he liked me. I was so different. No drugs, not that he took much of that stuff himself, and I was a straight-A student. He seemed to see something in me. He always wanted me around and that made me feel cool. Big.

... He seemed to see something in me ...

That line had hit Alexa the hardest. Because Logan claimed to see something in her too. He kept going on and on about how she was "real people" or a "hunter" or "one of the strong." In his sick philosophy, being "one of the strong" was the highest compliment. It meant you would assert your will on people no matter what the consequences.

It meant you were like him.

She thought about the times she had lost control, the times she had hurt suspects beyond what she needed to in order to subdue them. She thought about the dark satisfaction that brought her. Inflicting pain on evil people made her feel good.

But she wasn't like him. No way. She had seen what Drake Logan had done to his victims. It had taken all of Annette's scientific expertise to discover their identities. She had never done anything close to that and never would.

"Penny for your thoughts," Logan said.

She looked up at him, realizing she had been staring at the bare concrete floor, lost in thought.

Logan smiled, and in a voice surprising in its gentleness, said, "Come on. Tell me what's troubling you. You know I'll understand."

Alexa took a deep breath and finally forced herself to speak.

"You knew Powers."

Logan looked genuinely taken aback. "Wow. He actually told you that?"

"He didn't. Well, not exactly. He left me a journal in his will. It's mentioned in there."

Those pointed eyebrows went up a notch. "Oooh. I wish *that* was in the prison library."

"You hung out when he was in high school and you were a little older."

Logan nodded. "I remember him well, and that's more than I can say for a lot of those folks. Hangers-on and ass kissers, most of them.

Standing next to the sun and hoping it would make them shine. Proved useful, though. They'd do anything I'd tell them."

"Not Powers," Alexa said, her anger rising.

"No. Not Powers. That's what I liked about him. While the rest of that crew stood around all wide-eyed and hero worshipping, good old Robbie stood a little apart. Always had a look of a scientist examining something under a microscope."

"Like a bug," Alexa grunted.

Logan smiled. "More like a precious gemstone. He had never met anyone like me, none of them had. Hell, even I hadn't met anyone like me. For a while I thought I'd found a kindred spirit. I wasn't sure, though. He always seemed a little distant, like I fascinated him but he wasn't sure if he liked what he saw. So I decided to test him."

"What did you do to him?" Alexa demanded.

"To him? Nothing. We were at a kegger in the desert and there was this older biker guy. Big dude. Dumb as a post. Those kind of guys come in handy sometimes, though. He sure did that night. He was knocking back the J.D. and swaggering around and I could tell he was just spoiling for a fight. So I gave one of my lectures about the strong and the weak, and every time I mentioned the weak, or someone who put on a false front, I'd sort of give him a look like I was talking about him. It wasn't long before he got in my face. I whupped his ass right in front of everyone."

Alexa felt a chill. Her dead partner had mentioned this incident, but in his version the biker had started the fight. Logan must have goaded him so subtly that no one realized it had actually been him ratcheting up the tension.

She didn't doubt he was capable of it, even when he was much younger. Drake Logan was a born manipulator.

"Powers said you hit him in the kneecap with a rock."

"Sure did. He's got a good memory. Oh, what's that look for? That I didn't play fair? There's no such thing as a fair fight and you know it. The man that fights fair ends up getting beat one day. I've never been beat."

Alexa made an exaggerated look at the confines of his cell. Logan chuckled.

"You can never beat a real man by locking him up. Read *The Gulag Archipelago* by Solzhenitsyn."

"So what did Powers do after that?"

"Oh, I suppose he said he was disgusted and stopped hanging out with me. That's half true. He pulled away, and I was sorry to see him go, but I know I planted a seed."

"Yeah, he went into law enforcement."

"Sure, but with the seed. Does his journal mention any experiments?"

"Experiments?"

"Trying to get in the criminal mind. Stalking people or peeping in windows. That sort of thing. A man like Powers probably never crossed the line, but I'll bet you a million bucks he tiptoed up to it and peeked over at the other side."

Alexa grimaced. Logan was right. Powers had mentioned that a few pages later, when hunting an attacker who randomly mutilated people's faces, that he had walked around with a straight razor in his pocket like he was going to do the same thing. He had been horrified at how powerful and strong it had made him feel.

Logan leaned forward, forearms on his knees with the fingers interlaced. It was the same stance that Mrs. Brennan, her psychologist took when they got deep into discussion.

"So he did, huh? Wish I knew what he got up to, but I guess you won't tell me that. You never made any experiments like that, though, did you? No, you got an early start. I can tell. How did that come about?"

Smacking an older man who was trying to have his way with me with a horseshoe. Broke his jaw. No way I'd let you know that, scumbag.

Logan let out an exaggerated, mocking sigh. "Wish I knew. So much you could tell me that would make my time in here more enjoyable. But I'll tell you something, Alexa, I'll tell you what you came here to know. Powers was one of the strong. Not on our level, though."

"I'm not like you," Alexa grumbled.

"Ha! Yes you are. I proved it to the whole world. Remember that guy I sent after you? You disarmed him and then beat him within an inch of his life. And the look on your face! Damn, that made good television. Good thing he could speak enough to admit I was the one that sent you, otherwise you'd have lost your badge. You see how much I care, Alexa? I saved your job for you."

Suddenly Alexa found herself springing up from her chair and walking as fast as she could down the corridor. She couldn't take any more. She shoved past the two guards, who turned to stare at her.

Logan's mocking laughter chased her to the gate, where she shook the bars and signaled angrily to the camera.

"Open this damn gate, you idiots!"

Drake Logan laughed again. "Come back anytime, Alexa. We have so much to learn from each other!"

* * *

In the fifteen minutes it took to get back to the main gate, Alexa had managed to get her heart rate and breathing back down to something approaching normal. Her uniform was soaked with sweat, however, and she couldn't look at her escort, ashamed at her loss of control and what they might have overheard.

She had been a fool coming here. She had come to get answers, and had fallen into yet another Logan's psychological traps. He was a master manipulator, and could shape her reactions like putty in his hands.

And yet she kept on thinking about him. Why?

As she gathered her things with shaking hands, she automatically checked her phone.

Two messages. The first from Stacy, just a series of hearts. Instantly she relaxed. Not enough, but she sure as hell needed a reminder that there was goodness in the world. That improvement in her mood faltered a little when she saw the time Stacy had sent it. Right in the middle of math class. Well, Alexa never liked math either.

The second message came from Marshal Juan Hernandez, Alexa's commander at the U.S. Marshals service. Sent half an hour ago.

"Damn," she muttered, opening it. Hernandez was not the kind of boss who liked slow answers.

"Come to the office immediately. There's a new case."

"Damn, damn, damn," Alexa muttered. The office was clear on the other side of town.

She ran into the blazing Arizona sun and sprinted across the vast, baking parking lot to her Jeep.

CHAPTER FIVE

Alexa walked into the front office to find Stuart sitting and looking at his phone. He looked up at the same time as the secretary.

"You're late," the secretary said. "Nearly an hour late."

"Sorry. Work on the other side of town."

The secretary grunted, hit a button, and said, "She's finally here, sir."

Alexa winced at the "finally." Stuart got up and walked over to her.

"Sorry," she told him.

"No problem," he muttered, not looking at her. *Damn, he's mad too.*

"You can go in now," the secretary said.

They entered the Marshal's office to find Hernandez sitting behind his desk, the wall behind him arrayed with awards for valor and service and photos of him with two presidents and six governors.

Marshal Hernandez was a stocky Mexican-American with a thick moustache that was going gray just like his close-cropped hair. Deep worry lines were permanently etched into his weathered face, a legacy of thirty years of hard service.

"Sit," he said, indicating two comfortable leather chairs in front of his desk.

Hernandez studied her as they sat. After a brief pause, which only lasted a second but to Alexa felt like several hours, he said,

"There was a murder at Golden Greens Country Club last night. An attorney named Celeste Feinstein got stabbed to death in the garden a little before midnight."

"Feinstein? As in Feinstein and Garner?" Alexa asked. Feinstein and Garner was one of the leading law firms in the state.

"Celeste Feinstein is Maxwell Feinstein's daughter. She worked at another firm. She had been attending a social evening in the country club's ballroom for the past three hours. All the leading attorneys had been invited, as well as some other key staff such as accountants. Other than that, the only guests were a couple of golf celebrities. It's all in the file." Hernandez slid over a folder. Stuart and Alexa both reached for it. When her partner saw her reaching for it, he withdrew his hand.

Hernandez went on. "It appears someone jumped the fence on the edge of the property, cut across the green, and waited in the garden. When Ms. Feinstein went into the garden, he attacked and killed her."

Alexa flipped through the file, positioning it so Stuart could see. She passed several pages of information on the victim to photos of the crime scene. A blonde woman in her thirties lay on her back, numerous stab wounds to her chest and abdomen.

"The weapon used was a short-bladed knife. The killer stabbed her thirty-seven times, indicting a fury attack. No sign of sexual assault or robbery. Normally we would let the Phoenix P.D. handle a case like this, except that Homicide Detective John Rebstock noticed similarities to two other unsolved stabbing incidents, one last year in Phoenix, and another in Tucson two years ago. Both were young or youngish women with blonde hair wearing a red dress. Both also showed the same type of fury attack with a short-bladed knife, always stabbing in the abdomen except for a few defensive wounds."

"We got a serial killer," Stuart said. "Unusual for him to take so long between attacks. With that specific of an M.O., Rebstock would have found more if there were more."

Alexa nodded. Rebstock was an old-school detective who knew Arizona's criminal element like the back of his hand.

"He's widening the search to include the rest of the nation," Hernandez said.

"Any witnesses?" Alexa asked.

"Yes, but as usual no good description. When Ms. Feinstein didn't return from her walk in the garden, a couple of her colleagues went out to check on her. They found her. Then a couple of people recalled seeing a man they didn't recognize pass quickly from the garden through the ballroom before heading out the exit leading to the front hall. They describe him as a white male about six-two, athletic build, mid-thirties, short blonde hair. The two witnesses both noticed him because his blue suit was of too low a quality to be worn to an event of the city's leading attorneys, and one of his trouser legs was torn. We're presuming that happened when he hopped the fence. You had to have an invitation card to get into the event, and none of the employees recall him presenting one. Police are working with the witnesses on a composite sketch."

Alexa and Stuart exchanged a glance. Composite sketches weren't always the most reliable source of information, especially when the witnesses had only glanced at someone across a busy room after an evening of drinking.

Still, it was better than nothing.

She flipped through the rest of the file and came across the files from the previous two murders. Neither had any witnesses and so there were no composite sketches.

"So wait," Stuart said, "if he's going after blondes in red dresses, how could he be so sure Feinstein would come out into the garden? I mean, she had been there for hours, and that was the first time she went out there, right?"

"It appears so," Hernandez said. "Since we don't know when he jumped the fence, we don't know how long he hid out in the garden. It's a large garden and not well lit. He could have been out there for hours without being seen."

"But she might not have come out at all," Stuart said.

"True," Hernandez said, shrugging in a way to indicate he had no better idea than Stuart did.

"And why cut through the ballroom where he was sure to be noticed?" Alexa murmured. "He could have cut back across the green the way he came."

"I guess he wanted to be noticed," Stuart said. "What about security cameras?"

"None," Hernandez said. "They have a couple of security guards, but they didn't see anything."

Alexa shook her head. Rich people thinking their money made them safe. She'd seen this before.

"You better get over there," Hernandez said. "Rebstock is there now with the CSI team."

Alexa stood. After a moment's hesitation, Stuart stood as well.

Something's the matter with him? Alexa wondered. *Maybe it was the whole Stacy thing. Having the same name as that girlfriend of his who disappeared must have hit him hard. Poor guy.*

They headed out. Just as they reached the door, Hernandez called after them,

"Deputy Marshal Chase. A moment."

Stuart gave her a nod and left. Alexa turned back to her boss.

Hernandez looked uncomfortable for a moment, then grew serious.

“It has come to my attention that you applied to visit Drake Logan. Is that where you were today?”

Ugh. Never try to keep secrets from an officer of the law.

“Yes,” she replied, feeling like Stacy getting caught skipping class.

Hernandez muttered something she didn’t catch and shifted in his seat. “May I ask why?”

“He’s able to provide insight into the mind of a serial killer, and those who … might become one.”

“You are not currently on any investigation of Drake Logan or any investigation that requires Logan’s knowledge. In addition, you did this without consulting me.”

Alexa opened her mouth to speak, and found she had nothing to say. Her boss went on.

“I allowed you back on active duty because the need was so pressing, but on the condition that you see a counselor. Mrs. Brennan tells me you’ve been avoiding her calls.”

“I’ve been busy.”

And the three sessions I’ve had with her have been intrusive and annoying.

“Not too busy for personal maintenance. See Mrs. Brennan, and stop seeing Drake Logan. You’re too obsessed with that man. Yes, he killed Powers. I understand the struggles you’re going through because I’ve dealt with fallen colleagues myself. You’re only making it worse by getting emotionally entangled with that psychopath.”

Emotionally entangled? He makes it sound like we’re in a relationship.

“Sir, I—”

“This is an order, Deputy Marshal. Now I believe your partner is waiting for you.”

“Yes, sir.”

Alexa turned and walked stiffly out of the office.

* * *

Alexa noticed that Stuart remained quiet on the way over to the country club, and that he kept within the speed limit and didn’t rush through town with his usual Indy 500 driving style. He also didn’t stop to buy his girlfriend coffee.

Alexa didn't bother to wonder why. She was too embroiled in her own emotions. Stacy would be coming over to the ranch in a few hours after school and she really needed to be there to keep the girl company. Overlaid on that worry was Marshal Hernandez's little lecture.

And a strange feeling about the prospect of not visiting Logan again.

It almost felt like loss.

She shoved that odd thought aside as they parked in front of the rambling country club. Alexa surveyed the manicured lawn and vast glass front with disgust. How much water did they waste keeping the grass green? And how much electricity did they waste blasting the air conditioning to compensate for those south-facing windows? People came to the desert thinking they could live like they did in New England.

She and Stuart were greeted by a grim-faced security guard who no doubt had never had to deal with anything more serious than a drunken millionaire, and got escorted through a gleaming front lobby to the ballroom. Beyond that lay the garden.

Alexa had never been to Golden Greens Country Club before, and when she passed through the ballroom's double glass doors into the garden, she stopped in shock.

The garden looked like something from a European palace. It stretched out as far as she could see, with bushes sculpted into animal shapes, tall palm trees, and narrow paths winding their way through lush grass.

We live in a DESERT, people!!!

The bright yellow of police tape just visible through a gap in the foliage told them where to go. They walked down a broad central path between the topiary and cut right onto a narrower path leading to a pond.

Annette and her crew were busy in their white suits and face masks. While the suits kept them from contaminating the murder scene, it made them look like they were removing hazardous waste. The police tape had cordoned off an area about five yards around the pond. The body had already been removed.

They headed for Annette. Stuart muttered something under his breath.

"Hey, guys," Annette said, her face grim. "Not much to report, I'm afraid. It was breezy last night, so while we've collected several hairs, there's a good chance none of them are from the killer. The footprints on this gravel are faint and overlap each other. Of course the people who discovered the body walked all over it. The only material evidence we have is this."

She held up a clear plastic bag with a champagne glass in it. Water beaded on the inside.

"It was at the bottom of the koi pond, wiped of prints. Our guy was careful to cover his tracks. Hoping to get some DNA if he was dumb enough to take a sip. Saliva can sometimes adhere to a surface even if it's been submerged. He might have wiped it too well, though. He acted pretty calculating and careful."

"Except for passing through a busy ballroom when he could have hopped the fence," Alexa said.

"Yeah. Kinda weird. But figuring out weirdos is your job, not mine. There's another glass, with the victim's fingerprints on it, plus those of one of the waiters. No help there. The coroner will give you more about the stabbing, but from what I could see it was a blade about four inches long. Narrow. Looks like a switchblade. Imagine, a switchblade! I've only read about those things during training. This guy is old school."

"Where's Rebstock?" Alexa asked, looking around.

"Took a call and walked off. Oh, there he is."

Homicide Detective John Rebstock's bulky frame thudded down the path. Standing six-five and weighing at least three hundred pounds, he towered over the elven CSI expert and was almost as brilliant as she was at the job. He'd been in homicide as long as anyone could remember, and it had taken its toll.

The gin blossoms on his cheeks and swollen red nose told of long nights trying to drown out the things he had seen. His personal habits did little to help his appearance. His customary tan suit didn't look like it had ever met a dry cleaners, and he arrived in a funk of cigarettes and cheap aftershave.

Appearances could be deceiving. This man had caught more criminals than the rest of Homicide put together.

"There's been another murder across town," he said without preamble. "I think it's our guy."

Alexa felt a queasy feeling in the pit of her stomach. *Damn. This guy's moving fast. Too fast for us to stop him before he raised the body count.*

"Blonde with a red dress?" Stuart asked, speaking for the first time.

"Blonde but no red dress. Same sort of assault, though. Small-bladed knife, multiple puncture wounds to the abdomen, no sign of robbery or sexual assault."

"Two out of three is enough," Annette said. "I'm almost finished here. I'll catch up."

Alexa and Stuart followed Rebstock to the parking lot. As they left, Alexa realized Stuart and Annette hadn't exchanged a word.

CHAPTER SIX

That had been sheer torture.

Stuart had squirmed through the entire discussion with Annette, wanting nothing more than to sink through the ground all the way through the Earth's core and take up a career solving murders in China.

She hadn't even looked at him!

He had driven to the second murder scene in a daze, his mind replaying the conversation over and over again, searching for any sign, even the smallest indication that she had acknowledged him.

Nothing. Not a God-damned thing. She had switched off her feelings like switching off a light.

Stuart shook himself awake as they came to the next murder scene, one that couldn't have been more different than the first. No topiary or crystal chandeliers here, just crappy student apartment buildings near Arizona State University. In the parking lot they came across the familiar sad sight of an area cordoned off with police tape and a body shrouded by a sheet on the pavement between a line of bushes and a dumpster. A couple of city police stood nearby, keeping away a small crowd of curious onlookers, mostly of student age.

Rebstock led the way, totally in his element.

"What do we have?" he asked.

One of the officers turned to him. "The body was found just two hours ago. As you can see, it's pretty out of sight. It was totally invisible thanks to a truck parked right here," the officer pointed to an empty parking space that would have obscured the only line of sight to see the body unless you were right next to the dumpster. "There had been a truck parked here. The owner was the one who called it in."

They walked over to the body and the officer lifted up the sheet enough that they could peek underneath.

The woman looked in her early twenties, with a blonde ponytail and wearing jeans and a t-shirt from some local band. Her eyes and mouth remained opened in shock, her t-shirt a mass of blood below the breasts, where Stuart counted at least fifteen stab wounds. There were a couple on the right arm and hand as well, obviously defensive in nature. None on the other arm. Although she had struggled, she hadn't struggled for long.

Stuart winced. He hated it when the victims were that young.

The officer replaced the sheet.

"We already have positive ID from the wallet," he said. "Shelly Anderson. Twenty-two. Recent ASU graduate in sociology. Worked at Southern Bean Coffee Shop and volunteered teaching remedial literacy to children at risk. She lives in apartment 201 in this apartment complex. We've already spoken with the roommate. She doesn't know anything."

"You informed next of kin?"

"Yeah. They're in L.A. The parents are catching the next flight. They had no idea who would do this."

I do, Stuart thought. *Those knife wounds are just like the other victim's.*

"I think we should go to that coffee shop," Stuart said.

"I was planning on it," Rebstock replied.

"I got a hunch we should go there now," Stuart said. "Our guy might have been a customer."

And I sure as hell don't want to be here when Annette shows up.

* * *

Stuart's hunch proved correct as soon as they entered the Southern Bean Coffee Shop. All the employees wore red—the men had red t-shirts and shorts, the women with the same t-shirts and red skirts.

The three of them paused at the door. It was a large, bustling place, and the four servers stayed busy behind the counter serving customers, brewing up coffee, and chatting happily with one another.

It's her day off. They don't know.

Stuart took a deep breath. He hated this part of the job almost as much as the bodies. Ruining people's day. Perhaps ruining their lives. He didn't know how close any of these kids had grown to Shelly Anderson, but she will almost certainly be the first person they knew who got murdered. That wasn't something you got over.

He did a quick scan of the staff. Only one blonde, and he was a guy. Looked like a college kid. Nose piercing, some sort of tribal tattoo half-hidden by his shirt, and was that glitter around his eyes? All the victims had been women, but he wanted to talk to this guy just in case.

They cut to the front of the line, ignoring a complaint from a couple of hipsters.

"Excuse me, does Shelly Anderson work here?" Stuart asked, pulling out his FBI badge.

The baristas stared at it for a second. One of the girls asked, "Is this a joke?"

"I'm afraid not, ma'am," Rebstock said, pulling out his own identification.

"Homicide?" the blonde kid read. "Why … "

The kid fell silent. His coworkers all stopped to stare. The hipsters Stuart and his colleagues had cut in front of stopped talking too.

As Rebstock broke the news to them, Stuart studied each of the four employees for their reactions. The pudgy guy who had been laughing a moment before turned pale and leaned against the counter for support. The two Hispanic girls gasped and hugged each other, crying out something in Spanish. Maybe a prayer. Maybe sympathy. Maybe just an expression of horror. Maybe despair at losing their youthful innocence.

The blonde kid's reaction was the most interesting.

"Oh, crap. It was Crazy Charlie! I knew that guy would be trouble."

"Crazy Charlie?" Stuart asked.

"Yeah, a regular, or at least he was until I banned him." Stuart noticed he had "Assistant Manager" on his name tag. "He'd sit in that corner over there and stare at us. Creeped us out. But he never tried anything so I didn't have an excuse to get rid of him."

Stuart glanced over his shoulder at the table the kid indicated. "He sat over here? That's the furthest table from the counter."

"Yeah. That's why we never did anything. He would never get close or try to touch one of the girls or anything. We've had that before too. People think that just because you work behind a counter they can treat you like crap."

"What did he look like?" Stuart asked.

The shift manager shrugged his skinny shoulders. "Older, but not so old. Maybe early thirties. Looked like he worked out. Has blonde hair. Blue eyes."

The law officers traded a glance.

"Any visible tattoos?" Rebstock asked. "Scars? Accent?"

The shift manager and a couple of others shook their heads.

"No, none of that," he said.

"How long did he come here?"

"Every day for two weeks. I don't think any of us saw him before that." The kid glanced at his coworkers, who all murmured "No" or "I don't think so."

"Is Charlie his real name?" Rebstock asked.

"No. That's just a name we gave him. I don't know his real name. Anyone?"

He turned to his coworkers. None of them knew.

"So why did you finally kick him out?" Alexa asked.

The assistant manager bit his lip. "He approached me in the parking lot last week after my shift. He had been in his usual seat and left right after I did. Followed me, the creep. Came right up to me at the bus stop."

"What did he say?" Stuart asked. "Try to remember as much as you can."

"Ugh. I'll never forget it. He came up real close and said, 'Are you a woman?' And I'm like, 'No, creep, I'm a guy. Stop bothering us.' He just laughed and said. 'You sure you're not a woman? You wear glitter and guyliner.' And I'm like 'I'm gay, asshole. Got a problem with that?' I can't believe I said that. This guy's big, and I could tell he was psycho. There were other people at the stop, though, and it's a busy street. And he just made me so mad with all that crap."

"What did he do?" Stuart asked.

"He gave me this really creepy look, like really intense and angry, and said, 'You ever wear a dress?' and I'm like 'No.' 'You sure you're not trans?' And I'm like, 'No I'm not trans, and what if I was?' He just gave me that look again and said in this really low voice so no one else could hear, 'Then you'd be sorry.' Jesus, that creeped me out. I told him right then and there that he couldn't come back in the store, and if he did I'd call the police."

"How did he react to that?" Stuart asked.

"He turned and walked away. Like immediately. I thought I scared him off. I never thought he'd go after Shelly."

"Did he talk to or approach anyone else? Like Shelly?" Stuart asked.

"No, I don't think so."

"Just to order. Never said anything else," one of the young women said.

Rebstock cut in. “We’d like all of you to speak with a police artist in order to make a composite sketch.”

“Sure, anything,” the shift manager said. The others nodded, some wiping their eyes.

Stuart walked over to the corner table where Crazy Charlie liked to sit. He sat in the chair that could give him a view of the counter.

It gave him more than that. He could see the entire coffee shop, and looking out the floor-to-ceiling windows he could see the narrow parking lot and beyond that, a busy sidewalk. A good place to people watch. A good place to hunt for victims.

“He found himself a good spot,” Alexa said.

Stuart looked up. He hadn’t heard her approach. She stood by his chair so she could see what he saw.

“Another blonde woman wearing a red dress,” Stuart said. “But he’d have gone after that guy if he thought he identified as a woman. The hair color was what mattered. And the dress. Our guy specifically asked the shift manager if he ever wore a dress.”

“It’s like a red cape to a bull for him. I wonder why?”

“That’s for the shrinks to figure out. What I’m wondering is why he keeps revealing himself. He did it at the country club, and he did it again here. Killed someone at the place where he was a regular. He didn’t do that in the previous two cases.”

“No, he didn’t. It seems to be part of the escalation. Two murders nearly a year apart, and then a long break before killing two people in as many days.”

“Damn,” Stuart muttered, looking back at the counter where the staff were all hugging each other and crying. “That’s a pretty erratic escalation. I’ve never seen something like that.”

“Neither have I. With all these witnesses, though, I’m thinking we might get a good lead. Rebstock will put that information all over the evening news. If we’re lucky, someone will know who he is.”

“And if we’re unlucky?” Stuart asked.

Alexa’s face turned grim and didn’t reply.

She didn’t need to. They both knew the answer.

“How’s Stacy?”

Alexa shrugged, not looking at all surprised by the sudden change in topic. “It’s a bit touch and go at the moment.”

“You need to spend time with her?”

“Yeah, but—”

“Look, we’re in the data gathering phase right now, and so for the moment me and Rebstock can handle it. Why don’t you go back and see her?”

“But this case—”

“If anything comes up, I’ll call you. I promise. But you got someone who needs you at home.”

Lucky woman, he added silently.

“She’ll understand.”

“That’s precisely what she *won’t* do.”

Alexa sighed and rubbed her eyes. “This guy’s escalating like crazy. You’re right, though. I need to see her. I’ll work another couple of hours and then go home for a bit.”

“Promise?”

Alexa cracked a smile. “All right.”

Good. Because I don’t want you to lose someone you care about. Because then you’ll feel as crappy as I do.

CHAPTER SEVEN

It was time for the seven o'clock news, just a few hours after Alexa had visited the coffee shop where Shelly Anderson had worked, and now she was back home taking care of the other emergency in her life—Stacy.

The girl had been with the horses when Alexa returned an hour before, and had immediately run up to her, moaning, "They want me to see some stupid therapist!"

"Your parents?" Alexa had asked. She couldn't believe they'd be so proactive.

"No, the school! A therapist? I'm not some psycho. And the CPS came to our house."

Alexa tensed. This could change a lot.

This could change everything.

Not necessarily in a good way.

"So what happened? What did they say?" Alexa had asked.

"Stupid stuff," the girl had replied, throwing up her hands. "I don't want to talk about it. I have to give Smith and Wesson a currying."

With that, she had stormed off.

Alexa knew better than to go after her. Stacy would talk with her in time. Shaking her head, Alexa had gone in to make dinner.

Now Stacy had calmed down a bit and was doing her homework in Alexa's guest bedroom, which Stacy called "her room", while Alexa waited for Action News to start. She wanted to see how this would play. While she waited, she went through the old case files of the women who got killed in last year in Phoenix, and two years ago in Tucson.

There wasn't much there. The Phoenix victim was in her late twenties, an events organizer who got stabbed late at night in the parking lot after working on a local convention. Fifteen stab wounds to the abdomen and chest with a four-inch blade. No witnesses. The Tucson victim was in her early twenties and was returning from a date at one in the morning when she got killed at the door to her apartment building. Twelve stab wounds to the abdomen and chest, and two to the throat, all with a four-inch blade. No witnesses.

No witnesses in either case. There could have been, though. Both victims got killed in public places. While both attacks occurred late at night, they both happened in busy neighborhoods. The killer had taken an awful risk.

Risk must be part of it. It must give him a thrill. And now he's escalating the risk by deliberately creating witnesses.

That made sense. Contrary to popular belief, many serial killers can control their urges, at least part of the time. Assuming the Tucson killing was Crazy Charlie's first (the nickname had stuck in Alexa's mind and she decided it was as good as any), he had been able to stop for a while. The Tucson killing did seem like a first because he hadn't quite settled into the pattern. He had stabbed the throat a couple of times, and there were several shallow slash wounds after she had fallen prone, as if the killer was taking his frustrations out on the body.

That had changed with the second victim, who was killed only with stabs to the body, plus a couple of defensive wounds to the arms. Same with the later victims. And most times, the number of stabs increased. Not with the barista, but that had been the most public of them all. Perhaps the killer had gotten nervous or heard someone approach and needed to leave.

Not that it made a difference. The poor woman was still dead.

The killer always used the same small blade, what Annette thought was a switchblade.

Why? While switchblades could be easily concealed, would that matter to someone who already took so many risks? Or maybe he preferred it because it was small, that it took a lot of stabs to kill the victim. A stab to the throat would kill quicker, even with such a small blade, but maybe he wanted it to go on longer. The stab wounds to the throat on the Tucson victim would have each been fatal on their own. Maybe she died too quickly for his liking.

So an initial killing in a public place, followed by a year of nothing before another, more confident killing again in a public place. Then nothing for another year before two killings in two days, with the killer in both cases making sure there were witnesses. He even sat in a coffee shop for two weeks, acting in an obviously suspicious manner to make sure people would be able to describe himself.

And what about when he intercepted the shift manager? If the kid had said he identified as a woman, would Crazy Charlie have killed him right then and there in broad daylight?

The theme music for Action News interrupted her thoughts. She put away the case files.

Her sister-in-law Melanie appeared on the screen, her hair and makeup absolutely perfect.

Pity she didn't have a personality to match. She was as superficial as the day was long, and would do anything for a story. She'd been badgering for an exclusive with Alexa for ages, and had even had the gall to try and use Stacy to get to her.

"Breaking news!" Melanie announced in a chipper voice to which she tried and failed to add a bit of gravitas. "Police tonight are hunting for a potential serial killer who is suspected in the deaths of at least four women … "

Melanie went through the particulars of the case, detailing the murders of the four victims while showing a series of composite sketches. Alexa grumbled as she saw how different they were. One showed the suspect with jowls, the others with a lean or square face. Some showed his hair longer or shorter. Eyes wide apart or close and beady. The height and weight were all over the place too.

Most people make such bad witnesses.

"Are you working on this case?" Stacy said from the doorway. Alexa jumped a little. How long had she been standing there?

"Yeah. Don't watch this, Stacy. It's nasty stuff. Actually do watch it. This is what can happen when younger girls run away."

"None of them ran away, and they were all older."

"You increase your chances if you're a kid alone on the streets."

"I'm not a kid!"

Stacy's objection almost drowned out what Melanie's co-anchor said.

" … and your hero of a sister-in-law is on the case, isn't she, Melanie?"

"That's right," Melanie said, turning back to the camera and flashing her ten thousand dollar teeth. "Deputy Marshal Alexa Chase, my husband's sister, is leading the investigation. You might recall that she helped nab Drake Logan after he—"

"Jesus!" Alexa switched off the television.

"Is she allowed to do that?" Stacy asked.

"No."

"Are you going to sue her?"

"Shoot her? I'd love to shoot her."

"I said sue."

"Did you? I heard shoot."

"She called me this morning. I didn't pick up."

"Ugh. Don't pick up. Never pick up."

"Why did she call me after you told her not to?"

"She would have heard about you running away. We had an Amber Alert out for you, kiddo."

Stacy pulled a long face and sat down on the couch next to her.

"Are you still mad at me?"

"Yes."

"Sorry."

"Don't be sorry, just don't do it again."

"But I am sorry. I got you all worried. And you said that Stuart guy you like was hanging out at the Greyhound station all night."

"I don't like him. He's my partner."

"Suure."

"Let's talk about you. What's this therapist you're seeing."

That reminded Alexa that she needed to call Mrs. Brennan. Later.

"Just some dumb woman at the school. Everyone's going to see me going into her office. They're going to think I'm bulimic or something."

"Lots of kids go to therapy. There's nothing wrong with it. Have you gone yet?"

"Once. I have to go twice a week until she says I don't have to anymore."

"Did it help?"

"No. She just asked me about why I ran away and everything, and about my boyfriend. He got suspended."

Good. "That's too bad."

"Yeah, like you care. And CPS came to our trailer."

"I was about to ask about that. What did they say?"

"They said it was a routine check because I ran away. Asked me all sorts of stuff like if Mom and Dad did drugs or if Dad touches me or anything."

"What did you tell them?"

Nothing criminal was going on over at the Carpenter home. Alexa had checked. And double-checked. She had been itching for an excuse to come down on them, but unfortunately being drunk and useless isn't enough to get your kids taken away from you.

"That I didn't like how they drank all the time. She asked me if Dad ever drives drunk but he doesn't. He always drinks at home. Says bars are too expensive. They asked if they ever get mad and hit me when they're drunk, but they don't. They don't do anything."

They don't do anything. Like work. Or be parents.

"Did CPS ask about me?"

"Yeah. I told them about you being a US. Marshal and how I take care of Smith and Wesson. They said they might call you."

Alexa found hope spring into her heart, followed quickly by confusion. What was she hoping for? That they'd believe her when she told them Stacy had unfit parents? And then what? Stacy could move here permanently? Did she want that? Could she even handle that? Because that was the only option. The foster care system was too disruptive, and at times could even be dangerous. Predators lurked in some of those homes. Not many, the vast majority of foster parents were saints, but even if Stacy got lucky she might be sent to the other side of the city. Alexa would never get to see her, and Stacy would never get to see the horses.

Before Alexa could think of what to say, her phone rang.

Detective Rebstock.

"What's up?" she asked.

"We have a suspect. We're gearing up to go into his house. We already have a team monitoring the property and he's in there."

"Somebody called in already?" Alexa asked, glancing at the TV.

"Not from the news. A regular at the coffee shop who came in after we left got to talking with the staff. He knows the guy. Lives in a house next to the witness's apartment complex just down the street from the coffee shop."

"Damn. This guy really does want to get caught."

"Well, if you want to oblige him, get on over here as fast as you can. I'll send you the location."

"I'm coming."

She got up and turned to Stacy.

"Got to go. That case that was on TV."

Stacy looked disappointed. Alexa could tell she wanted to talk more. The kid had been working up the courage to talk ever since Alexa had gotten home, and now that she wanted to share, Alexa had to go.

The words of Alexa's brother came back to haunt her.

How can you take care of a girl like that when you're always running off on cases?

"I don't know how long I'll be but—"

"All night," Stacy grumbled.

"—but I'll try to get back before your bedtime."

The girl clicked her tongue and looked away.

Alexa put a hand on her shoulder. "Sorry."

"It's OK," Stacy said in a voice that made clear that it wasn't.

"Sorry. This guy's killed four people."

"I understand," Stacy said, not looking at her.

Alexa squeezed her shoulder and rushed out the door.

Stacy, bless her heart, does understand, Alexa thought as she ran to her Jeep. *It hurts that I'm always running off, but she does understand.*

The question is, how long will she remain understanding?

Because I'm breaking a promise right now. She ran away because I broke the implicit promise that my house was her house too. Now I'm breaking an explicit promise that I'd spend the evening with her.

But what the hell am I supposed to do!

Let's just hope I can crack this case before I accidentally crack this kid.

Something's got to change in her life, and soon. I just wish I could be around to make sure it will happen in the right way.

CHAPTER EIGHT

By the time Alexa made it to the residential street in northern Phoenix, not far from the coffee shop where Shelly had served coffee to her murderer, the cops were itching to make a move. She met with Stuart, Rebstock, and two plainclothes female officers around the block. It was a middle-class neighborhood of the poorer sort, with budget apartment complexes scattered amid two or three-bedroom homes.

One of the female officers filled her in one the situation.

"We've been watching the house for a couple of hours. His car is parked out front. The living room light has been on since we got here. A couple of other lights have switched on and off in other rooms. All the blinds are drawn so we can't see him or where he is in the house at the moment. We're assuming the living room since that's the only light on right now."

Alexa nodded. She recognized one of the officers as a specialist in dealing with sexual assault cases. Rebstock must have brought her along in case the perp had a hostage who required immediate attention. She hoped this officer wouldn't be needed in that capacity.

"So what do we know about this guy?" Alexa asked.

"His name is Brent Richter," Rebstock replied. "He's an electronics engineer and works for Rampart Security Company installing security cameras, burglar alarms, that sort of thing."

"Oh, great. A security expert. He might have installed hidden cameras to stalk his victims. That would explain how he knew where they'd be and when."

In addition to the regular security cameras visibly in place at various business, acting as a deterrent because people knew they were present, the industry also sold tiny models that could be hidden in numerous ways. Some were fitted with miniature transmitters to send their feeds to a receiver blocks away.

Rebstock nodded. "We're searching the murder sights now."

"Does Brent Richter have any history?" Alexa had to catch herself from calling him "Crazy Charlie."

"A couple of old ones. A barroom brawl five years ago where both men got cited but neither pressed charges. And for making threats two years ago."

"Threats? To who?"

"To a female waitress. He said she got his order wrong. She insisted that she gave him what he ordered and he flipped out, saying she'd be sorry for calling him a liar."

"I bet she's blonde and wore a red dress that night," Stuart said.

"Probably," Rebstock said. "The charges got dropped before it went to trial. I had to have someone at the records office dig to find those two incidents. Richter doesn't have a record, which is why Rampart kept him on. We haven't had time to interview his coworkers yet."

"So how are we sure this is our guy?"

"That regular at the Southern Bean Coffee Shop lives in the apartment complex right next to Richter's house. Turns out they have similar schedules and often go to the café at the same time. He's noticed Richter sitting in the corner table staring at the employees, and overheard them calling him Crazy Charlie. That stuck in his mind and then one day as he was coming out of his apartment he saw Richter doing some yard work."

"Bingo. Let's go." Alexa moved down the street. The homicide detective grabbed her arm.

"Got a Kevlar vest in your Jeep?"

"He's a gun owner?"

"A handgun and a rifle, both registered. That was the next thing I was going to say before you tried to bust in there and arrest him all by yourself."

Alexa gave him a wry smile and went back to her Jeep. By the time she had returned wearing her Kevlar, Stuart and the two female officers had geared up with vests of their own. One of the women carried a shotgun. Stuart had an M4 assault rifle he had convinced the local SWAT team to give him on long-term loan. Although Alexa was pretty sure that bent or broke regulations, she felt a lot better having the Iraq War veteran carrying the kind of weapon he fought with in the Middle East.

Alexa carried her standard-issue Glock. While she had trained with heavier weapons, she had won several pistol shooting awards and felt more comfortable with the sidearm. Rebstock did too, carrying an old-style revolver long after everyone else had switched to automatics. His colleagues laughed about it, but only in a teasing sort of way. The grizzled old detective was as dead of a shot with that antique as she was with her more modern weapon.

One thing that always worried her when going into situations like this with him was that he didn't wear Kevlar. Rebstock claimed they didn't make vests big enough for him. She knew for a fact that wasn't true. He just couldn't be bothered.

They moved down the street. Phoenix is a driving town and they saw no pedestrians. A man drinking beer on his front porch stared at them and went inside. A passing car sped up. None of them were in uniform and she felt sure 911 was going to get a call they had already been told to ignore.

They approached the target house, a small ranch-style house typical of Arizona. The front yard had a few cacti in it and was surrounded by a waist-high wrought iron fence with nasty looking spikes. That's all they could see because they stopped well down the street, out of sight of any security cameras the electronics engineer might have placed to monitor his home. They crouched behind an SUV parked in the street.

"We'll wait here until we can spring the surprise," Rebstock whispered. He pulled out a walkie talkie, pushed the transmit button, and whispered, "Do it."

Then he treated Alexa to a grin. "You got here late so you don't know the plan. You'll like this."

Stuart chuckled.

Alexa saw what they meant a moment later when a banged up old two-door Volkswagen Rabbit pulled up in front of the target house. When the driver got out, Alexa nearly had a heart attack. It was young blonde woman wearing a red skirt. She reached into the passenger's seat and retrieved a pizza box.

"Pizza delivery to the wrong house," Rebstock said. "Oldest trick in the book. People always open up, especially if a cute girl is delivering."

"Where did you find her? She doesn't look a day over eighteen, although she must be."

Rebstock chuckled. "Vice. She's a killer. Put her in pigtails and a Catholic school uniform and she'll collar a perv a shift."

"I can imagine."

The Vice squad officer went to the gate and tried it. To Alexa's surprise, it opened. Why have those metal spikes to warn off trespassers if you leave your gate unlocked?

She readied her gun. Something didn't sit right.

The girl in the red skirt walked up to the door and rang the bell.

Alexa and he colleagues waited, tense, quiet.

Nothing happened. No one came to the door. The fake delivery driver didn't say anything, so Richter wasn't speaking through the door. He simply wasn't responding.

She rang the doorbell again. No answer. She tried knocking. Same result.

"Screw this," Rebstock grumbled.

He got up and, hiding his revolver under his jacket, walked for the house. Alexa and the rest fell in behind him. Stuart got right behind Rebstock, hiding the assault rifle behind his prodigious bulk.

"Taking advantage of the terrain," he whispered when he saw her looking.

She would have laughed if the situation weren't so damn serious.

Rebstock didn't mess around. He went straight up to the front door, tried it, found it locked, and pulled out a set of lockpicks. Among his other skills, he was a certified locksmith.

Alexa stayed right at his side. Stuart and the officer with the shotgun positioned themselves at opposite corners of the front yard. The other officer disappeared around back.

A click of the lock, and Rebstock put away his tools and pulled out his revolver. Stepping to one side in case Richter decided to take a shot through the front door, he eased it open.

He was about to go in first when Alexa shoulder him aside and moved in herself. No way she was going to let an unarmored veteran take the lead.

"Police! Get on the floor with your hands behind your head!"

She ducked low and left, scanning the living room and seeing no one. The other officers streamed in after her. They branched out, checking the kitchen before moving on down the hallway to check the bathroom and both bedrooms. After a minute they ended up in the back yard.

Brent Richter wasn't home.

It didn't take long for Alexa to figure out how the lights were turning on and off in his absence. In the bedroom she found a vacation timer, the kind people used to make it look like they're home when they're not. Good for fooling potential burglars. And officers of the law.

The team set to work searching the house. Stuart found the handgun in the bedside table and the rifle behind the sofa in the living room. They found no unregistered firearms or drugs, although the fridge and kitchen cabinets were well-stocked with beer and whiskey.

"The man's got taste," Rebstock said, peering into the cabinet alongside her.

"What do you mean?" Alexa asked.

"Twenty-year-old Scotch. That label goes for a hundred dollars a bottle, and he's got three of them."

"A bit pricey for this neighborhood," Alexa said.

"I guess good booze is a priority for him," the homicide detective said.

The spare bedroom proved the most interesting. A work table was strewn with electronics, a soldering iron, and various tools and meters Alexa didn't recognize. They also found a couple of miniature cameras no bigger than her thumbnail and a metal box with an antenna that was marked "Repeater Number Three."

A repeater picks up a radio signal and rebroadcasts it, usually with amplified power. The police used them, as did all emergency services, to ensure clear communications in large, built-up areas. Placed on top of a roof, the signal from one of these devices could reach most of the city. His security job and a bit of fast talking could get him onto the roof of a tall building to install it. Anyone coming onto the roof later would assume the repeater was supposed to be there.

So Richter was boosting the spy cameras' weak signals so he could pick them up from the privacy of his own home, probably feeding the video into a computer. He could install cameras wherever he liked, sit back with a beer, and spy on his next victims.

Now she understood how Richter could know where his victims would be.

"Anyone find a computer?" Alexa called out.

A chorus of "no" came from the searchers. Alexa bit her lip.

"He's taken it with him," Alexa said. "That means he's probably monitoring another potential victim."

* * *

Back at the station, it didn't take long to discover where Brent Richter had disappeared to.

An officer came rushing in, one of Rebstock's best men.

"911 just got a call about another body," he said breathlessly. "A woman in her late twenties wearing a red dress."

They were out of the police station and tearing down the road in a heartbeat.

CHAPTER NINE

The woman lay on her back between a chain link fence and a large green pad-mounted transformer, the steel cabinets that regulate voltage for buildings, probably for the long warehouse of plain concrete a couple of hundred yards beyond the fence. The area was open, busy, and loud. On one side, traffic rushed by on a four-lane highway, and on the other, the roar of airplane engines came from the airport beyond the chain link fence and about half a kilometer of open ground.

He's done it again, Alexa thought. *Killed someone in public where he could be seen.*

It was a bit different this time, though. The woman was older, perhaps forty although Alexa had trouble telling through the heavy makeup and the worn features that had endured too much before the final humiliation of multiple stab wounds to the abdomen. The red dress this time was a red leather miniskirt with matching high heels. This woman was a prostitute.

If her appearance hadn't told Alexa this, the location would have. It was notorious for streetwalkers.

Alexa moved over to where a female officer was comforting another prostitute. This one wore a yellow leather miniskirt and matching halter top.

"How are you holding up?" Alexa asked gently.

The woman, trembling all over, simply shook her head, streaks of mascara down her cheeks.

"My colleague tells me you already gave a statement that you found the body and that you didn't see any suspicious characters. Please go back through your mind. Did you see anything at all that seemed out of place?"

"No, nothing," the woman said in a hoarse whisper.

"Anything. Even if you think it's not important."

She shook her head, staring at the pavement but not seeing it. "No. Nothing. Just a normal night. I ain't even been out here that long."

Alexa pulled out printouts of the composite sketches.

"Have you seen this man?"

The prostitute looked at them. “Oh, the man on TV. I heard of him. That’s why I don’t wear my red dress no more. No, I ain’t never seen him.”

Alexa surveyed the scene. The cars sped by. Even with parked police cars and a crowd of officers, few people slowed to stare. This was an arterial road with no reason to stop. People simply hurried through her on the way to somewhere else. The prostitutes hung out here because there was a wide shoulder, making it easy for Johns to pull over and discuss terms of business. It was also well away from residences whose owners might complain to the police.

She tried to imagine the scene. Richter’s vehicle, a late-model black Lexus they still hadn’t located, could have pulled up to the victim. He parked, got out, and suggested a quickie behind the transformer. It was a good seven feet tall and as long as a minivan. Plenty of room to hide. It might even have been the reason the woman had been standing there in the first place.

So Richter had stabbed her, risking getting spotted once again, and then vanished.

But this location seemed strange. It wasn’t downtown like the other murder sites. And while it was visible, it didn’t carry as much of a risk of getting caught. Plus the population was transient, and Alexa doubted Richter had hidden a camera here.

She imagined that Richter had been driving by for some other reason, and that by pure chance he had spotted a blonde woman in a red dress. That triggered something in his sick mind, he pulled over, and …

So an unplanned killing. But if the killing was unplanned, what was he planning to do here?

Rebstock lumbered up, phone in hand.

“We found his vehicle.”

“Really? Where?”

Rebstock pointed. “Half a mile down the road on the opposite side. There’s an abandoned light industrial park there. He hid the car in that. Good thing I set out a search pattern or we’d have never spotted it.”

“So he’s close. How long do you think the victim has been dead?”

“Rigor mortis hasn’t set in, so less than three hours. Actually a lot less. Richter’s engine was still warm.”

“It’s a hot night. It could stay warm for an hour.”

“An hour isn’t very long. He’s around somewhere.” Rebstock’s weary eyes scanned the surrounding night, as if the murder would emerge like a phantom from the shadows.

Alexa looked across the street. Nothing but empty lots and a distant gas station. She could see a squad car parked out front, the officer no doubt questioning everyone inside if they had seen anything.

Why abandon his vehicle?

Alexa spun around to the chain link fence and the hangers and cargo planes beyond.

“He’s gone in there! He’s going to get on a plane. Where do these planes go?”

“All over,” Rebstock said. “Mexico and cities in the Southwest mostly.”

Alexa ran back to her Jeep, picking up Stuart as she did.

“Where are we going?” Stuart asked.

“Driving down the road here looking for holes in this fence. He’s close, but if we don’t hurry he’s going to get pretty damn far!”

They hopped into Alexa’s Jeep and drove along the shoulder against the traffic as Stuart leaned out of the open passenger-side window, shining a flashlight along the fence. Beyond it, immense cargo planes taxied down the runway or stood on the tarmac, their backs open, forklifts carrying crates driving up the ramps before disappearing inside.

They only got a quarter of a mile before Stuart shouted, “There!”

Alexa slammed on the brakes, making Stuart half fall out of the window. “Easy!”

“Sorry.”

Alexa peered out the window as Stuart scrambled back in, cursing to himself. He sure was in a bad mood lately. Usually he’d joke about something like that.

What she saw outside her Jeep was no joke, though.

A hole had been cut through the fence. A pair of bolt cutters lay in the dirt just inside.

I bet he left his fingerprints all over those. He’s taunting us.

He doesn’t know how close behind we are, though. So he’s going to change his tune pretty damn quick.

Alexa got out of the car and ran to the gap. She ducked through, Stuart following close behind and calling it in.

Once on the other side of the fence, they paused. They had no idea where to go.

A few hundred yards ahead lay the runway, with a heavy cargo plane just beginning to taxi for takeoff, lights flashing in the night. Far to the right stood a row of brightly lit hangers. Between them and the hangers stood a plane getting loaded with cargo. It was an open, well-lit space. She could see every distant figure as clear as if it were broad daylight.

Everyone seemed to be occupied with various jobs, and no one was shouting at or pursuing an obvious trespasser.

"Damn it. Where is he?"

"If he's going to hop a plane," Stuart said, pointing, "that one being loaded is the best bet."

"Unless he's already hopped one," Alexa grumbled, already running for the distant plane.

By the time they had sprinted several hundred yards in the warm desert night, both were sweating and panting, especially Stuart in his regulation FBI black suit and tie. She really needed to talk to him about changing his attire to suit the climate.

The workers overseeing the loading stopped to stare.

The partners pulled out their badges.

"U.S. Marshal! FBI! Have you seen any suspicious characters in the area? We're hunting a well-built blonde man in his thirties."

The workers exchanged looks.

"No, we haven't seen anyone."

Alexa pointed at the plane. Its engine was off and its cabin dark.

"How long has this been sitting here?"

"A couple of hours."

"When did you start loading it?"

"About an hour ago."

"Was the back open before that? Before you came here to work?"

"Sure, but—"

"Everyone out of the plane!" Alexa ordered, already sprinting up the ramp.

She nearly got run over by a forklift backing out. She was about to shout at the driver until she realized he was only obeying her instructions.

Stuart's right. I do need to take it easy.

Once the forklift and a couple of workers went down the ramp to stand staring curiously at the two officers, Alexa and Stuart drew their guns and entered the plane.

The interior was a vast metal enclosure with a high, arched roof. The front of the cargo hold was already filled floor to ceiling with heavy crates on pallets. Closer to the back, and to them, was a jumble of crates and smaller boxes that hadn't been organized yet.

Lots of places to hide.

Alexa and Stuart leveled their guns and walked quietly forward, eyes and ears alert. They didn't announce their presence. With all the ambient noise, Alexa hoped that if he was hiding in here, Richter hadn't heard them arriving and ordering everyone out. That way they could surprise him. If he had heard, then he was obviously not planning to give up.

So they paced forward, their footsteps silent beneath the background roar of airplane engines.

A cluster of boxes on the right was their first obstacle. Stuart stopped just ahead of it, covering Alexa as she edged as far as she could to the left to stay out of knife range, then swung around to see behind it.

No one.

They continued forward. Beyond the first cluster of boxes was a jumble of smaller containers, including a large bag marked U.S. Mail. Alexa could spot half a dozen places Richter might be hiding, and unlike the stack they had just examined, there was no way to check them from a distance.

If he pops out, I'll shoot him. There's no time to negotiate, not with someone like that.

Just then, they heard a soft rustling coming from behind a pile of boxes.

Alexa and Stuart froze.

The rustling came again, softer and briefer this time, as if a body was changing position.

As if getting ready to strike.

As near as Alexa could figure it, the rustling sound came from just behind a pile of boxes sitting in the middle of the cargo plane. Just in front and to the right stood a stack of boxed-up radios encased in clear plastic wrap on a wooden pallet. To the left were stacked several rolls of something wrapped in yellow plastic.

Alexa and Stuart moved around the stack of boxes, her close to the rolls, and him having to squeeze between the pallet of radios and the stack. If Richter sprang up, knife in hand, they'd both be within easy stabbing distance. Alexa promised herself not to let that happen.

They swept around the stack at the same time, and groaned.

Inside a cage was a medium-sized dog, drugged for flight, that shifted on its blanket in half slumber. It rolled on its back, twitched a leg, and then shifted back on its side, not a care in the world.

A quick survey of the rest of the plane revealed nothing. They checked the cabin too. Also nothing.

Brent Richter had given them the slip. Again.

How many lives is this going to cost?

They hurried out of the plane, where the loading crew stood in a small huddle.

Alexa turned to an older man holding a clipboard, assuming he was in charge. "Did you load the last plane?"

"Yeah."

"When did it leave?"

"It just took off like twenty minutes ago. I don't think anyone could have snuck aboard."

Alexa wasn't so sure about that. Richter seemed adept at getting away with just about anything, even in the most public spaces.

"What about other planes? How many have you loaded in the past three hours?"

The supervisor hesitated, then flipped through the pages on his clipboard.

"Five, including this one."

"Five! Where to?"

"Going from the one that left twenty minutes ago backwards," the supervisor ran his finger down a list, "their destinations are Mexico City, Dallas, L.A., New York, and another to Mexico City."

Alexa cursed.

"If he got on one of those cargo planes, he could be anywhere by now," Stuart said. "Look, here comes Rebstock and the others. We'll need to search the airport, and contact the pilots of those planes."

The supervisor checked his clipboard. "Mexico City, Dallas, and L.A. should have landed already."

We've lost him, Alexa thought. *He could be anywhere by now.*

CHAPTER TEN

The search of the airport was fruitless. None of the pilots or the airport security in the cargo planes' destinations found Richter, and Alexa and her team ended up back at the police station, desperately trying to find a lead.

"All four destinations he could have gone to are major hubs," Alexa said as she and Stuart worked side by side in the office. "If he managed to sneak onto a second plane, he could be anywhere."

"I'm checking that," Stuart said, not looking up from his computer. "From what I'm seeing, if he snuck aboard a cargo plane within one hour of landing on the first one he took, he could be in … " Stuart kept tapping away. "Ugh. Five different Mexican cities, eight U.S. cities, and in the air heading for three cities in Europe. Or he could have snuck out of the airport at his first destination."

And the longer we don't find him, the more of a chance he has to go even further.

"Where in Europe?" Alexa asked, a thought bubbling up from the bottom of her mind.

"London Heathrow, Amsterdam Schipol, or Munich International."

Alexa turned to Rebstock, who had just hung up the phone across the room. Calling across the busy workspace, she asked, "Have you found any family information on Richter yet?"

"Yeah. He was born in Germany to a serviceman station there and a German woman. He holds dual nationality but he's lived in the U.S. since he was a child. One brother in Thailand and a sister in Rhode Island. Both parents are deceased."

Alexa snapped her fingers. "Munich. I bet he went to Munich. He must have extended family there."

"That's a bit of a reach," Stuart said.

Alexa shrugged. "Yes it is, but what else do we have to go on?"

"The fact that he's got a personal fortune," Rebstock said.

"A personal fortune?" Alexa asked.

Rebstock smiled, walking over to them so he didn't have to shout over the other officers busy at work on other cases. Because even though a serial killer was on the loose, the police still had to deal with their regular round of robberies, drug deals, and barfights.

"That was the next thing I was going to mention before you interrupted with a highly speculative but, knowing you, correct assessment of where Richter fled to. Besides checking his family, I decided to check on his finances. Haven't got a warrant for his bank details yet, but I don't need to. Remember that expensive Scotch in his house? And his late-model Lexus? And the house he owns free and clear? Well, he can't afford that on thirty-five grand a year."

"Only thirty-five?" Stuart asked, "for a security engineer?"

"Assistant security engineer," Rebstock corrected. "He's only been at that job two years and just finished his training. His boss tells me he came to the job with no experience, but was a quick learner and worked hard."

Alexa gasped. "He took the job to learn the skills."

"That's right," Rebstock said. "Not sure where his money comes from, but I've learned that car and the house are completely paid for. No way he did that on thirty-five. I haven't tracked down what other jobs he had. I will, though."

"If he's got money, that will make it a lot harder to track him," Stuart said.

"Once I get the warrant to look at his account, I'll put in a request to freeze his assets. As you know, checking for overseas accounts and getting those frozen will take time. Far too much time. And who knows what kind of accounts he might have tucked away in tax havens somewhere. We need to get on him now."

"We need to alert Interpol," Alexa said.

"Already done," Stuart replied.

Alexa smiled. It was good working with professionals who thought as quickly as she did.

"We need to especially alert the authorities in Munich," she added.

Stuart nodded. "You know what? Richter must have had it planned it in advance. He probably got access to the cargo plane schedules somehow—working for a security company it wouldn't be too hard—and picked his murder spot accordingly."

"He couldn't have known a blonde prostitute with a red skirt was along that stretch of highway," Alexa objected.

"Maybe not. Or maybe he'd seen her out there before and controlled himself. Or maybe he timed it that after his first two murders, he'd escape via the airport and, on the way, kill the prostitute if she happened to be at her usual spot."

Alexa sighed. "This guy is hyperorganized. And I got to ask, if he took the job with Rampart Security just to learn about hidden cameras and repeaters, I wonder what other skills he's picked up along the way."

"We're working on is job record," Rebstock said. "So far, nothing. I'm thinking he arrived in Arizona shortly before the first murder. He got the job with Rampart a couple of months after. I've talked with his boss and he says Richter was a quiet employee. Kept to himself but was an eager learner, always asking for more information, asking to borrow manuals. That sort of thing."

"We need to get this guy," Stuart muttered. "I'll inform the FBI office in Germany. They can liaise with local law enforcement."

He picked up the phone, hesitated, and looked at Alexa.

"You want to go, don't you?"

Alexa blinked. "To Germany?"

Stuart nodded as emphasizing the obvious. "Yeah, to Germany."

The possibility caught her by surprise. "Do you think we could?"

"Maybe. Agents from some of the divisions get to travel a lot. I can talk to Deputy Director Sandford."

Sandford ran the FBI's Behavioral Affairs Unit and had helped launch the experimental joint task force with the U.S. Marshals Service to fight the alarming rise in serial killings across the United States. The experiment so far involved only her and Stuart. They'd solved four cases so far and so Stuart probably felt he could call in some favors.

Alexa suddenly grew doubtful. "We still don't know he fled to Germany."

"It's a logical theory, and in the time it takes us to get the FBI's gears in motion, we'll know more."

"Go for it," she said.

He nodded and dialed, murmuring under his breath, "I need to get out of this damn town for a while anyway."

Alexa cocked her head and stared at him.

What's that all about?

She didn't have time to think about it, because his mention of getting out of town prompted a thought of her own.

She'd be leaving Stacy alone.

* * *

It was late by the time they got their proof, and their permission.

Rebstock had dug into Richter's financial records and search history, calling in several favors to get the warrants fast-tracked. That involved getting a judge in night court to approve the warrant, and then waking up the president of Richter's bank to have him access the records. Rebstock had been on the Phoenix P.D. for so long, he could get these things done.

What he discovered confirmed Alexa's suspicions. When Richter opened an account at an Arizona bank, he had done so with funds wired from Deutsche Bank, the largest bank in Germany. That got Rebstock to wondering why he hadn't transferred funds from whatever local U.S. bank he had been using before, and when he checked for bank accounts under Richter's name, he found that Richter had another bank account in Savannah, Georgia.

"I'm still working on getting access to that account," he told them as soon as he found out. "Savannah P.D. says that in the last year that Richter lived there, they had three cases of blonde women getting stabbed. No fatalities, but all in public places."

"Were they wearing red?"

"They didn't keep a record of that, unfortunately. But they do have a composite sketch."

He held up a printout. It looked a lot like the composite sketches the Phoenix witnesses had made.

Now we're getting somewhere, Alexa thought.

The homicide detective also discovered that he had been right in his hunch that the suspect was a relatively recent arrival in Arizona. He had briefly rented a luxury apartment in Tucson, with no visible means of support, around the time of the first murder. Just two days after killing her, he broke his lease, losing his security deposit in the process, and moved to Phoenix.

"Sounds like a panic move," Alexa said when he told her and Stuart. "Just like the wounds on the first victim show he wasn't sure of himself, once he had done the deed he wanted out."

"But why not flee to another state?" Stuart asked.

Alexa shrugged. "Maybe he likes the region. Maybe he couldn't resist staying in Arizona so he could still run a bit of a risk of getting caught. That seems to thrill him, and he'd lose that if he ran off to Illinois or someplace."

"He sure is running now," Stuart said.

"Because now he knows he's being chased. He wants to be seen, but he doesn't want to be caught."

"Want to make a bet that once he settles down in the old country, he'll be stabbing Germans just as happily as he was stabbing Americans?" Stuart asked.

"I won't take that bet," Alexa grumbled. "Because I think you're right."

Stuart got back on the phone to the FBI, and told them what they had learned. Alexa watched he spoke to his supervisor, saying only "yes, sir … yes, sir … I will sir."

Alexa paced. Why couldn't they come to a decision already!

Stuart hung up the phone and smiled. "The information about the bank convinced them. Looks like we're going to Germany. They're booking us a direct flight from Dallas first thing in the morning. There's a red-eye from Phoenix leaving in two hours. Just enough time to pack."

* * *

Alexa was in such a hurry to get home and throw a few essentials in her bags that she didn't even think of Stacy until the lights of the Carpenters' trailer became visible as she drove up her own driveway.

Then she cursed a blue streak to herself. She had promised to talk to the kid before she went to bed, but now both her ranch and the trailer had their lights off, the only lights remaining on were the outside ones around both dwellings that burned all night to dissuade prowlers.

"I hope she's not too mad at me," Alexa muttered, then added silently, *She'll sure be mad when she hears I have to go to Germany. I promised I'd stick around and spend time with her.*

Alexa went inside and found Stacy gone. No note. She checked her phone and found the girl hadn't texted either.

As she packed, Stacy's absence nagged at her thoughts. That silence was unlike her. If Alexa couldn't get off from work in time to see her at the time she said she would—and that happened at least a third of the time, reminding Alexa that she should really stop making promises—then Stacy would usually send a goodnight and an unhappy emoji. She'd been far more patient with these little disappointments than most thirteen-year-olds would be.

It looked like that patience had come to an end.

Alexa cast a nervous glance out the window toward the Carpenter trailer, worried she might have run away again.

No, she reassured herself. *Her parents would have called. Even they aren't* that *irresponsible.*

Alexa hurried with her packing. She had just enough time to catch that plane.

But no matter how much of a hurry she was in, she couldn't help feel troubled that she was abandoning the kid just a couple of days after finding her.

Just a couple of days after promising her that she wouldn't leave.

And that made her worry. What if Stacy acted out again, and this time she wasn't around to take care of the problem?

She pulled out her phone and wrote her a long text, explaining the situation and apologizing several times while saying she could stay over at the ranch anytime she wanted, or every night if she needed. She didn't have to tell her parents Alexa was away.

Alexa pressed "send", wishing she had said enough and knowing she hadn't.

She just had to hope it would be enough to keep her from running away again. At the moment, there was nothing more Alexa could do.

CHAPTER ELEVEN

"They're getting too big for their britches," the senator grumbled.

"We never thought there'd be a whole string of cases dropped in their lap," the FBI man replied, his worried voice an octave higher than the senator's. "We gave a rise in serial killings as a justification, but the numbers keep rising! It's giving us the opposite kind of exposure. If this keeps up, they'll be able to ask for more funding. Get more agents. Their own offices. Who knows? Maybe a distinctive badge. And then where the hell will we be? This game is enough of a headache already. We can't afford another agency diluted our power base."

"You're ranting," the senator said in a dismissive tone. "It's still in its early phases. If we cut it off now, it won't cause much of a ripple. Our friends in the national press have been treating the cases local news and have skipped over it."

"No they haven't!"

"Sure, Drake Logan hit the headlines. That was unavoidable. But the rest of the murders? Some regional papers and websites have tucked it in the back pages. We can't expect them to ignore it completely. Blood sells, after all. But they've downplayed the teamwork between the two agencies."

The FBI man gave a nervous laugh. "I like how they've been ignoring our press releases. Our PR people are furious and don't know what's wrong."

"You see? Just relax. We'll take care of this in due time."

"The sister-in-law has been screaming to corporate to let her kick the Phoenix stories to a national level. She's got a human interest angle. The Deputy Marshal took in some teen junkie or something."

"And we've blocked that story. She's nothing to worry about."

"I wouldn't be so sure. The news business is strapped. They've been losing out to the Internet for years. A big story like this would rake in the cash. They'll be tempted."

"We've spoken to them. That won't happen." The senator's voice had grown impatient, as if explaining something to a dull child for the fifth time.

"What if she goes to YouTube with it? Or one of the outlets we don't control?"

"Then she'd get fired. It's in her contract. No moonlighting."

"Still … "

"Let's worry about the main danger, which is these two having another success. The reports say this latest sicko acts like he wants to get caught. Any way we can stop that?"

"Stop what?" the FBI man asked, dumbfounded.

"Stop him from getting caught."

"You seriously can't expect me—"

"I expect you to do what you need to do for the team."

"I don't have any control over some murderer who's probably fled the country!"

"No need to squawk. Of course you don't. Just slow down the investigation somehow."

"How? It'll seem obvious."

"It's your house, keep it in order!"

The FBI grew angry, although he still couldn't quite hold his voice level. "Look, I've had enough of this disrespect. I've done my part and—"

A third voice cut in, wavering with age and yet still carrying the heavy weight of authority. "You will both work together on this. Be as subtle as possible. We cannot allow any attention or suspicion to come our way. If the two agents still manage to get their man, you need to find fault with them somehow. Look into their lives. That sister-in-law might be a good asset. That's why I didn't let you request her dismissal."

"Character assassination can backfire," the senator said. "We'll try to make them look bad in the field."

"All right," the FBI man sighed.

"Firm up," the old voice commanded. "A lot is at stake here, and I expect you to do what's necessary."

"Yes sir," the senator and the FBI man said in unison.

The last thing they heard before the line went dead was a series of three electronic beeps, muffled as if in the background of one of the callers.

* * *

Stuart yawned his way through a cup of bad airport coffee as they waited to board their plane from Dallas to Munich. Its burnt taste and fake milk didn't help his mood. He had been checking his messages every ten minutes, and still nothing from Annette.

Well, almost nothing. When he got approval to go to Germany—something he still couldn't believe he actually pulled off—he had texted her the news. Then, just before he hit send, he added, "I hope we can talk after I get back."

Stuart knew it for a bad idea even as he was writing it. That didn't stop him, though. He needed to figure all this out. He needed answers.

That was twelve hours ago, and she still hadn't replied.

OK, the be fair, eleven hours and twenty-seven minutes since she read it, but isn't that enough time to reply?

Almost nothing? Worse than nothing!

Maybe she's overworked with the three killings. She's the best, so Rebstock would have put her on the Richter case for sure. She's probably just pulled an all-nighter at the crimes scenes and morgue.

Get real! She's done that before and texted you.

"You all right?"

Alexa's voice pulled his out of his thoughts. She had just come back from checking the departure time.

"Yeah, just tired." *You wanted someone to talk to, remember?* Pause. "Just trouble with Annette."

"Oh, that's too bad. You two all right?"

Stuart tried to make his shrug casual. It came out exaggerated.

"Nah, we're fine. It's just that I think we want different things. I don't think she's serious enough for me, you know?"

"Not serious? I've never seen someone more serious about her job."

"Her job? I'm not talking about her job!" he exclaimed. "There's more to life than the job."

He glanced sidelong at Alexa, who looked like she had taken it personally. "Sorry."

"It's OK," Alexa said, although Stuart wasn't convinced. "It's not like I haven't heard it from everybody else. So what *is* she not serious about?"

"Oh, I don't know. It's just that outside her job, everything's just one big party for her. She didn't take our thing seriously."

"You've only been dating her two months. Maybe she doesn't want something serious."

"But why not?"

Alexa gave him a sympathetic smile. "That's just how Annette is. She's like a magpie, looking for the next shiny thing."

"Oh, great. So I was the next shiny thing. That's just frickin great."

"Sorry."

"So you're telling me she goes through lots of boyfriends?"

"And girlfriends, yes. She's a social butterfly. The few times I've gone out with her it's always been a different circle of people. And she acts like they've been friends for life but I know she barely knows them."

"Yeah, I kinda sensed that," Stuart grumbled. "Especially the friends part. In the past two months with her, I've met so many people, but hardly any of them twice. She said she broke up with me because she could tell I wanted to get serious."

There was a pause. Stuart stared at the tile floor of the waiting area. Alexa seemed at a loss for words.

After a moment, she nudged him with her elbow. "Hey, I thought it was guys who were supposed to be afraid of commitment."

"That's what I said!" They both laughed.

Once they stopped, Stuart smiled at his partner.

"I really shouldn't be so torn up about it. In my gut I knew it was going to be like this. Right from the start I knew it. I guess that made me overcompensate. Anyway, I'm being selfish. How's Stacy doing? She's not going to give me another heart attack, is she?"

"She felt so bad about putting you through that trouble. She says she's sorry."

"She doesn't have to be sorry as long as she doesn't do it again."

Alexa grimaced. "I feel bad about taking off for Germany. I promised her that I'd spend more time with her, get her through this rough patch. And here I am about to head off to Europe for God knows how long."

"She understands. Remember that weekend I was up at your dad's ranch?"

"Which visit? The time you fell off the horse twice or the time you fell off only once?"

"Hilarious. You should do standup. Anyway, she told me that she's proud of what you do."

Alexa flushed. "Really?"

"Yeah."

"She actually said proud?"

"Yes, she did. She really admires you. I bet she feels awful about what she put you through."

"She better," Alexa grumbled. "I just wish I could be around more. All the problems that led to her running away are still there."

"I'm not sure you can solve them, Alexa. Her parents aren't going to stop drinking and suddenly act like real parents. We've both seen enough deadbeat moms and dads to know that. And as she gets older she's going to grow more and more independent."

"Yeah, but this kid was seventeen!"

"Her parents know. Her teachers know. I think that danger is passed."

Alexa made a rueful smile. "Her dad chased after the kid with a shotgun but he had forgotten to load it."

"Nice one. I wish our suspects were like that."

"Speaking of, let's see if Rebstock has sent us an update." She pulled out her phone.

You really can't stop thinking about work for five minutes, can you?

"We were taking about Stacy," he said.

"She's in a sulk. I was just getting her out of it and this happens. Oh, look! He did send us a message."

Stuart leaned over her shoulder to see her screen. They read together.

"Munich confirmed. The airport there reports that a worker unloading the cargo plane got knocked out and his uniform taken. Another of the loading crew saw an unfamiliar man matching Richter's description driving a forklift at high speed for the employee entrance, wearing a poorly fitting employee uniform. A key card swipe from the card stolen from the assaulted worker shows Richter used that entrance to get out of the airport. The man on security at that entrance was new and so didn't realize Richter didn't work there."

"Great," Stuart said. "Now that guy's loose in Germany."

They read on.

"I also confirmed Brent Richter's movements for the past few years. He spent two years living in Richmond, Virginia, where he had no visible means of support but was active in kickboxing and Judo studios … "

Oh, wonderful, Stuart thought. *Now we have to worry about getting beaten up as well as cut.*

" … and earned blackbelts in both martial arts. Obviously he had prior training. No one earns black belts in only two years. Before that he lived in Chicago, where his brother lived for a time before buying property in Thailand. Looks like they overlapped. Still haven't discovered what he did there. We're trying to contact the brother. He's not answering calls. The sister in Rhode Island says she hasn't talked to Brent for more than five years. She seemed reluctant to talk, like she was hiding something. I've contacted Homicide up in Rhode Island to bring her in and lean on her.

"That's it for now, kids. I'll send you more when I have it. Drink some of that good German beer for me and don't do anything that I wouldn't do."

The gate crew announced that boarding was to begin. They got up, gathering their carry-on bags.

"You should check your phone too," Alexa said.

Stuart smiled. "And you're always complaining that Stacy is a phone zombie." Nevertheless, he pulled out his phone.

Sure enough, there was a message from Deputy Director Sandford.

His boss was succinct, as usual.

"We've cleared everything with the FBI and local law enforcement. You will be allowed to bring your firearms. Airport security will load them onto a secure locker on the plane and the authorities in Germany will hand them back to you. When you make it to Munich airport, meeting you will be Astrid Rilke, an officer from the German federal police. She will assist throughout your mission.

"The eyes of two agencies are on you. Be careful and be successful."

Stuart cocked his head, surprised at this last line. Well, of course the FBI and the U.S. Marshals would both be watching their new collaboration take on its first overseas case. They'd been down to Mexico, but that was a common thing for both agencies, especially the Marshals. It was less frequent that either agency went to Europe. But did the deputy director really need to point this out to an experienced agent?

And what about "be careful and be successful"? He'd been working under Sandford for years and the man had never said something like that. Being careful was drummed into you since day one of training. Being successful was equally obvious.

So why say it?

Maybe Sandford was hinting at something. This collaboration was of an experimental nature, after all. After a move across country and four successful cases, Stuart had begun to forget that. Could it be that the collaboration might be threatened with cancellation?

It seemed hard to believe considering their batting average, but it wouldn't be the first time he'd seen a good program terminated and the funding diverted to some do-nothing program that only wasted money. He worked for the federal government, after all.

"Get anything?" Alexa asked as they got in line.

"Sandford has a local contact waiting for us."

"Good."

Stuart almost added the rest, then stopped himself. No need to worry her about something she couldn't control. She'd go all out to solve this and any other case. Let her concentrate on that, and the high-drama home life she'd built for herself.

Besides, he told himself. *We've been doing great together. Once we bag this guy, it'll be five in a row. How could they cancel us after that? Don't get worried over nothing.*

But as they boarded the plane, Stuart kept wondering about Sandford's strange, maybe even coded, message. And thinking about it brought up an old memory, just a passing incident, but he had a feeling it fit somehow.

If only he could remember it. Something he'd heard when he was still back in D.C., a snatch of an overheard conversation between to other deputy directors as he walked down a hallway in headquarters late one night and a door had been left open a crack. Someone saying something about Deputy Director Sandford …

CHAPTER TWELVE

The instant the plane landed and she was able to turn on her data, Alexa checked her messages. She grimaced to see no message from Stacy. No message from the girl's parents, either. She knew they had her number, and on the way to the airport in Phoenix she had spoken with Stacy's mom. Alexa had told her she was going away, and that if there was any trouble to call her immediately. The mother, sounding half asleep from the cheap bourbon she drank and the television she stared at all day, had promised they would.

But would they? Would they even remember to?

The only other message was from Astrid Rilke, the officer from the German federal police staying she was waiting at the gate.

The passengers started shuffling forward down the aisle. Yawning, Alexa grabbed her bag. Stuart was still checking his phone. Alexa almost asked, then from the look on his face knew the answer.

Poor guy. I knew Annette would be too much for him.

Stuart wasn't the right fit for Annette. Alexa had seen that right off. He was a laid-back, fairly serious guy who obviously wanted some stability in his life. She'd seen that with people who had served in warzones. Law enforcement was full of them. They either acted crazy, partying like college students, or they looked to routine and a reliable circle of people around them. That's what Stuart needed.

And that's what he wasn't getting. The move must have been tough for him, and he probably leaned on his new girlfriend too much for a social life rather than building one of his own.

Not that Alexa was one to judge. She hadn't had a relationship in a few years, and she hardly ever saw her friends. Between work, the kid, and the horses, she didn't have any time.

And she didn't have any time to figure out how to fix that, because waiting for them at the gate was a back-uniformed female officer with short blonde hair and sharp blue eyes above high cheekbones. Alexa waved and she and her partner moved over to her.

"Welcome to Bavaria," she said in measured, perfect English. "I am Polizeihauptmeister Astrid Rilke, Bundespolizei."

They shook her hand, Alexa figuring that “Bundespolizei” meant “federal police”. She had no idea what a Polizeihauptmeister was, though. Her rank? She had four stars on her epaulettes, anyway.

Stuart greeted her in German, and for a moment Alexa felt left out as they traded a few sentences in a language she had never learned.

She hadn’t known he spoke any German. She supposed it had been on his CV and she hadn’t remembered because she didn’t feel it was significant to working in the Desert Southwest. Now Alexa felt a bit useless.

After a moment, he turned to Alexa with a smile. “Sorry, just wanted to see if I still remembered my German. I picked some up when I was stationed here.”

“It is still quite good,” Astrid said. She raised a heavy satchel. “I have your firearms. There is a mountain of paperwork you need to fill out for this.”

“Some things are the same the world over,” Stuart said.

“Come, I will get you up to date in the car. We have been making our own investigations into Herr Richter and have found that his family owns some property not far outside Munich. We can investigate once you have settled in your hotel.”

“Let’s go now,” Alexa and Stuart said at the same time. They glanced at each other and laughed.

“Very well,” Astrid said, a tight smile briefly appearing on her own lips. “I will explain the situation in the car.”

A blue and white police car waited for them just outside the terminal. Alexa noticed Astrid didn’t have a partner waiting. Apparently the German police only felt the case was worth assigning one officer.

Stuart whistled. “A BMW. You guys drive with class.”

Astrid grinned. “We like to live well here in Germany.”

They got in the car and were soon out on the highway speeding east. Astrid explained the situation.

“About forty-five minutes from here is a country estate owned by the Richter family. They are quite a prominent family here in Bavaria. Judges, lawyers, local politicians, although most now live outside the country to pay fewer taxes. Brent Richter’s mother was a countess.”

“We heard he married a serviceman,” Alexa said. “An odd move for a countess.”

“Well, he was a major in the Army and went to Yale, but yes it did cause a scandal. The family all but disowned her, and from what we’ve learned from former servants and neighbors, they took out their anger on the boy.”

“Abuse?” Alexa asked.

“No sign of that. Merely rejection. His father and mother never got invited to family functions, and neither did he.”

“Charming,” Alexa grumbled. She was getting really, really tired of hearing about uncaring families. Then a thought occurred to her. “But now he has money. Where did that come from?”

“The mother had some of her own, as did the father. Both are now deceased. We’ve discovered, however, that there was an uncle, a financial investor who was disillusioned with the family as was his sister, Brent Richter’s mother. He never talked to any of them, his sister included. He didn’t seem to take a side in the scandal about her marriage. He wasn’t talking to any of them at that point. So it must have come as a surprise to everyone that when he died five years ago, he left all his money to a nephew he had never met.”

“Our suspect,” Alexa said.

“Yes.”

“Five years ago is just about when Richter began his wandering,” Stuart pointed out.

“Perhaps he had these fantasies bubbling inside him for a long time,” Alexa said. “Most serial killers do. And he finally got the means to do something about them.”

“Yeah,” Stuart agreed. “A lot get caught because they don’t have the means to move town or hide out. Richter can move from country to country. He’s probably got money stashed in all sorts of places.”

“Two different banks in Germany and one in Switzerland,” Astrid said. “That we have tracked down. We’ve heard he has an offshore account in one of the Caribbean tax havens. We’re tracing that now, although we might not be able to freeze it like the European accounts.”

“You were able to freeze the Swiss bank account?” Alexa said.

Astrid glanced at her in the rearview mirror. “Surprised? The Swiss aren’t being as secretive and closed as they used to be. They’ve added some oversight and are willing to cooperate with the police, at least with a common criminal such as Richter. If you’re trying to freeze the assets of a Third World dictator, you won’t even get the banks to answer your calls.”

"So is Richter at this estate now?" Alexa asked. "Who else lives there?"

"It's not generally used and there are no full-time staff. A groundskeeper comes three times a week, and a maid once a week. At the moment, no one is staying there."

"That we know of," Stuart said.

"Exactly," Astrid said with a curt nod. "Which is why we are going to check. It is the nearest safe spot for Richter after fleeing the airport. As far as he knows, law enforcement isn't aware that he's even in the country. And if it wasn't for your tipoff, we wouldn't have known. The attack on the cargo crew would have been simply a mystery."

They drove in silence for a time, Alexa and Stuart both checking their phones. She didn't get any messages, which made her down. Dwelling on it made her feel even more down. Glancing at Stuart out of the corner of her eye, she could see he was getting the same disappointment from his phone.

Maybe I should move far enough into the desert that I don't get cell phone coverage. Life would be a hell of a lot more peaceful.

After leaving the glittering high rises of Munich behind, having not even caught a glimpse of the old historic center so familiar from tourist photos, they entered the countryside. Suburbs soon gave way to cultivated fields, which soon gave way to dense woodland.

"Hey, look!" Stuart cried and pointed out the window.

Visible through a break in the trees was a large castle of gray stone standing atop a steep-sided hill. It had four tall, round towers, each with a red gabled roof. A flag with the emblem of a double-headed eagle snapped in the breeze from one of them.

"Is that where we're going to?" Stuart asked.

Astrid laughed. "The Richters are new money. They made their fortune in the war."

"Which one?" Stuart asked, more bluntly that Alexa thought necessary.

"The first one. They kept their fortunes through the second, though. They were Nazis by convenience. Like many wealthy German families, they shifted politics to whoever was in power."

"What are their politics now?" Stuart asked.

Astrid gave a little shrug, not taking her eyes off the winding country lane hemmed in by trees on both sides. They had left the highway and it felt like, other than the paved road, they had dropped back a century.

“They don’t involve themselves in politics anymore. As I said, they mostly live overseas, in Latin America or Southeast Asia or North Africa, where their money can buy them more and the authorities don’t watch over them as closely.”

“Do some of them have a criminal record?” Alexa asked.

“Nothing serious. Drunk driving. Disturbing the peace in nightclubs and bars. I spoke with their local police and heard nothing but glowing praise. I called some private individuals and they painted the picture of an entire family that lives for indulgence.”

“Why the glowing praise from the police?” Alexa asked.

“Not bribery,” Astrid sniffed. “We’re not like the American police. No, it’s just that the local police take their orders from the local elite, and such a wealthy family such as the Richters are good for the town economy, even if they don’t stay at their estate so often.”

Alexa barely heard Astrid’s explanation, stunned as she was at the German officer’s casual assumption of police corruption in America. She’d obviously been watching too much Netflix.

They passed through a small town, looping around a small fountain in the central square surrounded by buildings with wooden beams and gabled roofs, a postcard village from another time. That illusion quickly vanished as they continued down one road, passing a modern supermarket and a community activity center. A crowd of laughing teenagers, hair wet from swimming, burst out of the front door laughing. Briefly Alexa wondered why they weren’t in school and then remembered it was the weekend.

The weekend, when Stacy stays up all hours, and still no text from her. She’s either seriously depressed, seriously angry at me, or both.

They left the small town behind and came to a stretch of open fields. Behind a dry stone fence, a dozen horses grazed on the lush grass.

On impulse, Alexa asked, “Could you stop for a second?”

“Um, all right,” Astrid said, obviously confused. She pulled over on the narrow shoulder. Alexa could barely open the door without risking scratching it on the rough stone wall.

Once out, she plucked a cluster of tasty looking flowers growing on the shoulder, and reached over the fence.

A couple of the horses looked at her quizzically, then ambled over. She pulled out her phone.

"You're a natural mother!" Stuart said.

Alexa looked over her shoulder at him and blushed. *Natural mother!?* "That girl is so horse crazy maybe this will make her ease up a bit."

"I'll take a couple of shots too. She hasn't ghosted *me* yet."

"She hasn't ghosted me either!"

"Yeah, she has," Stuart said, lifting up his phone.

"One day doesn't count as ghosting."

"It does at her age. Don't worry. She'll come around."

"Since when have you become an expert on teenagers?" Alexa asked, as she grabbed another bundle of flowers for the horses to munch on.

"Since partnering up with you and hearing about them constantly," Stuart replied, taking another picture.

Astrid leaned out the window. "Are we solving the case or playing tourist?"

Alexa and Stuart traded a look, both annoyed and embarrassed. They walked back to the car. As Astrid shook her head and put it into gear, Alexa started sending photos and ignoring their local minder. Alexa didn't like her attitude. She could have at least asked why they had stopped instead of assuming they were just playing around.

They went another mile, then turned down an even narrower country lane enclosed by towering oaks. Their branches spread to reach over the lane and almost touch those of the tree on the other side, making it feel to the passengers like they were passing through a tunnel illuminated by an ethereal green glow.

The lane dead-ended in a pair of stone towers ten feet high, each bearing a sculpted crest on the top. Between the towers was a wrought iron gate. A two-door Volkswagen was parked in front of it. An older man with a weather-beaten face and wearing a loose shirt, gray cap, and trousers worn and dirty at the knees stood by the gate. He gave a brief wave as the police car pulled up.

The man came to Astrid's window as she opened it and they briefly spoke in German. The man looked at the two Americans curiously for a moment, and then went to the gate and opened it with a set of heavy keys.

“That is the gardener,” Astrid said. “He hasn’t been to the estate for two days.”

“No electronic system, no visible burglar alarm, and no cameras,” Alexa observed.

“There is little crime here,” Astrid said. “Not like in America.”

“Except for the serial killer,” Alexa said.

“The American serial killer,” Astrid said.

“The German-born serial killer,” Stuart corrected. Alexa elbowed him and flashed him a quick smile when Astrid wasn’t looking.

The gardener opened the gate and they drove inside a few yards. He pulled his own vehicle in, closed the gate behind them, and together they continued.

The forest soon opened up, and Alexa took in a quick breath as to either side a vast lawn spread out to a distant tree line. At the edge of the trees to their right, a small herd of deer grazed on the grass. Up ahead, the lane stopped at a large circular drive around a stone fountain, dry at the moment, in front of a three-story stone mansion that looked like it had been built in the previous century.

As they drove up, Alexa’s gaze roved over the grounds and the building. No lights. No open windows. No vehicles.

Wait, what was that? Tire marks in the grass to the left of the building. Alexa pointed, and Astrid nodded as if she had already seen them.

They stopped and got out. Alexa noted that while the groundskeeper kept the flowerbeds in decent shape, weeds had cropped up in a few places and the immense lawn needed cutting. Also, the house needed some repairs—a cracked window, flaking paint on the door, and a couple of rotted wooden slats on the gabled roof.

Stuart asked a question in German to the gardener, who asked something back. Stuart repeated, and the gardener answered.

“No one has visited this house in nearly a year,” Stuart said, looking around. “Makes me wonder why they keep it.”

They headed for the left side of the building, where they could now clearly see the tire marks of a car that had passed through the tall grass, heading for the back of the building.

Just as they got to the corner, a woman’s scream cut the quiet air.

It sounded like it came from behind the mansion.

CHAPTER THIRTEEN

Alexa whipped out her pistol and rushed for the back, heart beating fast, eyes alert for the slightest hint of danger.

"You're not allowed to draw your weapon without a clear threat!" Astrid said, running beside her.

"Brent Richter is a clear threat."

Stuart seemed to agree because he pulled his sidearm too. He didn't have the M4 he had borrowed from the SWAT team. Back in the States, he had briefly considered trying to bring it along and decided not to create an international incident at the airport.

The way alongside the building was hemmed in by the wall and a large cluster of shrubs, so that the driver would have had to drive carefully. It soon opened up into a broad back yard with an empty pool, a covered Jacuzzi, and a scattering of bushes and sculptures. A yellow Jaguar convertible was parked by the empty pool with its top down.

The three of them stopped, confused at not seeing anyone.

Another scream. It sounded like it came from behind a large bush.

A young woman, completely naked, rushed out from behind it. She ran screaming, looking over her shoulder, her long red hair trailing behind her.

Emerging from a bush came a hulky blonde man who ran after her, slowed down by having to hold his pants up. The end of his belt swung in time with his steps, the buckle catching the sunlight.

"Halt!" Astrid shouted.

The man glanced at them, swore, and ran for the Jaguar, which sat only a few feet from him.

Stuart shouted something in German and pointed his gun. The man ignored him. Alexa cursed. If he didn't stop, they couldn't fire.

Alexa aimed for the tires as the Jaguar ground its gears and shot toward them in reverse.

She didn't get a chance to shoot, because Astrid ran into the line of fire. The German officer had holstered her pistol, drawn her nightstick, and charged at the approaching vehicle.

Alexa watched, amazed, as the woman leapt into the low-slung car, timing it perfectly so she didn't get hit by the fender, instead landing in the passenger's seat right next to the suspect. The driver raised his hands, the Jaguar swerved, forcing Alexa and Stuart to jump out of the way.

Alexa stumbled in the tall grass and heard a crash. She spun around and found that the Jaguar had banged up against the back of the house. Astrid stood inside, beating the living daylights out of the driver.

She rushed over, Stuart at her side. The driver pleaded something in German, cringing at the assault. Alexa wrenched over the door and threw the suspect face down on the grass. He didn't resist. Probably all he wanted to do was get away from Astrid.

"Gotta love German efficiency," Stuart said, putting a knee on the man's back as he cuffed him.

Alexa looked around for the victim and saw her standing in clear view just a few paces away, still naked. She started shouting something in German, shaking her fist.

"It's all right," Alexa said in a soothing voice, hoping she could understand English. Alexa holstered her gun and moved over to her. She pulled off her jacket to put around the woman's shoulders.

The woman shoved her away and shouted something that definitely sounded like a swear word.

"What the hell?" Alexa said.

"She's telling you this was consensual," Astrid said, hauling the man to his feet.

"It didn't look consensual to me," Alexa said.

"It is the rough sex," the man said in heavily accented English. Alexa blinked. All those years in the United States and Richter wasn't fluent?

Unless …

"What's your name?" Alexa asked.

"Dieter Weiss. What is going on? Why did you arrest me?"

"Why did you run? Only guilty people run."

"I panicked. The German police are brutes, like you just saw." Weiss rubbed his forehead to emphasize his point.

Alexa paused. While this looked like more or less like the man in the police sketches and the ten-year-old driver's license photo they had retrieved, the confidence with which he spoke sounded a lot more convincing than the many "I'm not him" lies that suspects had given her over the years.

Astrid reached into his pocket. The suspect smiled and said something in German in a tone that told Alexa exactly what he was saying. Female officers have to deal with the same things no matter where they work.

Astrid pulled out a set of keys and a wallet. As she searched it, flipping through a large wad of cash, Alexa kept an eye on the naked woman, who showed no signs of being embarrassed by having Stuart standing almost in front of her. To his credit, he didn't stare.

Astrid pulled out a photo ID, held it up to the suspect, and said, "It looks like this isn't who we are looking for. I'll have to run a check on him to be sure this card isn't a fake."

She rummaged through the wallet some more, pulling out several more cards, all in the name of Dieter Weiss. Meanwhile, the woman spoke to her in rapid, angry German.

"She swears it was consensual. Just rough sex and play acting," Astrid said.

Alexa slumped. It looked like chasing down Richter wasn't going to be so straightforward. She turned to Weiss.

"What's your connection to the Richter family?"

"I am their accountant. Taxes. Investments. I come here to play with my friend."

"That didn't look like playing," Alexa growled.

The accountant laughed. "You live boring life."

"Do the Richters know you're here?"

"Sure. I have a key to the gate. They say I stay whenever I like. It is good for this old house not to sit empty."

Astrid barked a question at him. He replied in an angry tone, gesturing at the bruises around his head. Astrid said something and jerked her head toward the Jaguar that nearly knocked them all down. Weiss laughed again in his annoying, superior way and gestured to the keys she had taken from his pocket when she searched him.

"He has keys to the house," Astrid said. "A least we don't have to break in."

Alexa chuckled. "Sounds good. But could you try to stick to English? I don't speak German like my partner."

Astrid gave a nod that left Alexa the impression that she had received the message but would only act on it if she felt that way.

Take the bad with the good, I guess, Alexa thought. They went to the door, Astrid and Weiss in front, Stuart coming just behind, and Alexa with the woman, who with Alexa's permission had retrieved her clothing, torn and tossed everywhere, from behind the bush. She carried them, still naked, across the front lawn to the door with the rest of them.

"Make her put something on," Stuart said. "You know how liable this makes me?"

Astrid stopped and smiled. "I forgot, you are from the country of lawsuits." She snapped an order to the woman, who sneered and started to dress. Astrid glowered at her for a moment then turned back to face Stuart. "Nudism is common here in Germany."

"I remember the Tiergarten," Stuart said with a smile. "But this is an arrest situation."

The woman got dressed, Astrid checked her ID and radioed in an update to the local station, and then mounted the broad stone steps and unlocked a large door with an ornate fanlight and brass fittings. It opened into a darkened hallway that smelled of dust and lack of use.

Weiss led them though the ground floor, where several rooms had dusty sheets draped over the furniture. The kitchen was stocked with fresh groceries enough for the couple to last the weekend, plus alcohol enough to last a squad of marines a month. Upstairs was the master bedroom, shut up and dark, and several guest rooms, one with the couple's clothing.

"We choose this one because it has Jacuzzi," Weiss said, still taking it all as a joke.

While Astrid guarded the couple, Alexa and Stuart made another search of the house and grounds, from the stuffy attic to the cellar with its impressive racks of wine. Nothing.

Brent Richter hadn't fled home. He had vanished somewhere else.

"How far could he have made it by now?" Alexa asked the German policewoman once they returned from their pointless search.

Astrid frowned. "Assuming he came on the cargo plane into Munich, which he must have given the attack, then he could be just about anywhere in Germany by now. Or further. We have a good rail network here, and the Richter family has many properties, some under other names or their shell corporations. We haven't tracked them all down yet."

“We’re going to need to,” Alexa replied. “He’s killed three times this week in Phoenix alone. He’s accelerating faster than any killer I’ve ever seen.”

“Maybe it’s no accident he fled back here,” Stuart said. “Maybe he wanted to come home for his final murders.”

Alexa nodded. “Yeah, that makes sense. And he likes the risk too, so he’ll be killing soon. As soon as he sees an opportunity.”

CHAPTER FOURTEEN

Brent Richter could not believe his luck. He was back in Europe. Back home. Back to the place of beginnings and endings.

Because it was ending. All of it. He knew that. Knew it and accepted it. On one level, it sort of made him feel relieved. The constant rage consumed and exhausted him. At times he got so bitter about everything he'd stagger and need to sit down to catch his breath. All his life. All his life like this. Raging and snarling and aching to get back at those people.

They all deserved it. Every single one of them. All right, not all. All but one, the only other one who saw what he saw, endured what he endured without become corrupted like his brother or sister. The only other star in the dark night.

Oh, that's poetic, Richter smiled as he walked down a street in the old historic center, exuding an outward air of calm as he passed beneath a streetlight before passing into shadow. He was good at pretending to be calm. Good at hiding.

So nice to be back in Europe. Good food, a familiar language, fine art and architecture. The place of poets. And he was a poet too. Not with weak words to make women and pseudointellectuals swoon, but a poet with how he lived his life.

Out of darkness and despair—poetry.

Damn, you really are getting sappy! Must be because you're getting to the end. Enjoy the ride. It isn't over yet.

Richter chuckled. This was the way to live. Right at the edge, but the real edge. Not some artificial one. Drugs and the booze had never worked for him.

Why are you wasting your life away like that? his mother would screech. *You're only twenty! Partying all day and night! Do something. Just for appearances. University. Take a part of our business. We'll put someone under you who'll make sure everything works fine.*

Richter ground his teeth. Yes, he had tried every substance he could get his hands on back then. None of it could block out his mother. None of it took that screech out of his inner ear. None of it took away the laughter of his older siblings as they egged on their mother's bullying.

Now he had something that would silence that screech forever. Silence the laughter too.

Not right now, though. He had to keep his cool. A short walk to the metro, then five stops, then get on the bus for five stops and he'd be at a storage unit facility in the outskirts. A change of clothes, a wad of cash, a burner phone, and a set of keys that would open up so much.

Until he got there, he had to stay cool. Richter took deep breaths as he walked along the nearly deserted street flanked by narrow houses built in the nineteenth century. The sidewalk was far too well lit, making him stand out like a beacon, and he still wore the clothes he'd worn when he had escaped on the cargo plane. They were rumpled, smelled like the fact that he hadn't taken a shower in two days, and he had a big grease stain down the side of his shirt and another on the right knee.

He looked like someone in trouble, and people notice trouble. Especially in a quiet, safe neighborhood like this one.

Twenty minutes, he told himself, glancing to the right and left, alert for anyone looking out a window or coming out a door. *Then you'll be at the storage units and you can breathe easy. Grab one of those hats while you're at it. More security cameras on European streets. Some things are easier here, like having good public transport to get you some place anonymously. Some things harder, like stabbing a woman to death in public.*

"Adapt to local customs," his older brother Hans always said. *"You'll get away with a lot more that way."*

Hans had sure followed his own advice. At the age of twenty-eight, his face already bloated by alcohol, had stumbled onto a jet to move to Thailand and make his hobby a way of life. This after taking Brent to a season's worth of swinger's parties and exclusive clubs as a sort of warm up.

Hans always tried to act chummy, but Brent would never forget he had taken his mother's side when Brent was still young and vulnerable. He had fumed all through that season while his brother plied him with alcohol and women, fumed and remembered.

Brent Richter was not the kind of man to forget an insult.

Hans, his usual clueless self, didn't even notice.

Paradise is just a month away, he had told Brent one night, as they watched an erotic stage show that members of the audience were allowed to join, *but I'm getting mine while I can.*

Whenever they went to a party or a sex club, the two brothers would split at the door, Hans soon finding a partner or partners and disappearing into a back room for hours, while Brent hung around the common areas, sipping a drink and watching it all with mild interest slowly overcome by crushing boredom.

He had indulged, of course. Brent Richter had his basic needs, he had to admit. Disliking women didn't mean he disliked sex. It was all so fake, though, pretending that there was nowhere you'd rather be than in bed with that person or people. Such temporary joy. No real thrill.

The worst night, the final night, he had gone into a private room with this young blonde, a silly shop girl impressed by Brent's Rolex and refined drink orders. He'd always hated blondes, the dumbest of an inferior gender. His mother had been a blonde, of course. It explained a lot about her character.

When he and the shop girl got into it, and she was moaning beneath him, or at least pretending to moan, his face buried in that blonde hair, he had felt the rage rise up stronger than it had in years. Suddenly he felt disgusted by the creature in the bed with him. He wanted to crush her, stamp her out of existence like a bug.

Before he knew it, his hands clasped around her throat. The woman's eyes went wide, her body rigid, and Brent jerked his hands away like he had been electrocuted. He leapt out of bed, stammering an apology.

"Don't stop," she cooed. "I like it."

Like it? You're not supposed to like it. That takes away the *fun!*

He walked out of the room without a word.

And his brother wanted to dedicate his life to stuff like that? Hans Richter was a drunk and an idiot. Good thing Brent hadn't talked with him in years. The chump would have sold him out the moment the police called, just to cover his ass.

"You want to turn out like your big brother?" His mother would screech any time Brent got a call from a girl or tried to go on a date. *"You want to embarrass your parents by making us go down to the station and bail you out too? You know how much we had to pay that girl's parents? And stay away from men too. Don't think I don't know what your brother gets up to in North Africa. You turning out that way*

would be just what we need. God, why did we ever have kids if they're just going to torture us! The biggest mistake of my life!"

That stopped his feeble attempts at having a normal youth. It didn't matter. Brent wasn't all that interested in dating beyond satisfying his primal needs. He had never socialized much, never really joined in with the fake games of rearranging the hierarchy that boys constantly do. He was amazed that, as an adult, he had become so good at charming people. Like that lawyer he killed in the country club garden. She had no idea she was in anything other than a perfectly ordinary conversation until Brent stuck his knife in her gut.

Brent's hand strayed to his pocket, where he felt the welcome, reassuring weight of the switchblade. As a teen, when he wasn't ducking out of the house for long nighttime walks of blissful silence away from the screeching, he'd watch movies in his room. His parents had given him a TV for his room for his tenth birthday, saying, *"Now you don't have to bother us in the living room."*

He loved action films. War, gangsters, Westerns … anything where men fought other men and the strongest came out on top.

Then he discovered the gang movies of the 1960s and 70s. Tough groups of youths just a little older than him, always with a leader even tougher than the rest. Those had been rough times—some American cities had decayed so much they looked like something from Syria or Iraq—but they had been simpler times too. The gangs didn't fight with UZIs and Glocks, they went into a rumble with a bit of two by four, or a length of pipe, or that king of old-school street fighting, the switchblade.

What an weapon! Folds up in your pocket and is so slim most people don't notice it. Those that do think it's a vape. And so out of fashion that when you pull it out, people don't even know what it is until you press the button and that razor-sharp blade pops out.

Just four inches long, but of strong steel that won't chip or snap if you hit a rib. And it takes a lot of thrusts to kill them. That's the best part. Just like in those old movies. He remembered one epic fight between two bikers where the last whole five minutes of the film was them slicing and stabbing at one another, their leather jackets providing some protection, both men dodging and weaving, but slowing as each took hits. By the end of that fight, the victor emerged a staggering red ruin to collapse in the arms of his fellow gang members. As the credits rolled, you had no idea if he lived or not. If he died, it didn't matter. His last moments were epic.

Almost to the metro now. A man crossed from a side street ahead. Brent's eyes tracked him as he hurried across to the metro stop and jogged down the steps. Brent slowed. He wanted that guy well ahead of him so he didn't catch a look at Brent's face. Some people were bound to see him down there even at this hour, but the fewer the better.

Emerging out of the pool of light around the metro station staircase came someone who made Brent stop in his tracks.

A young woman, barely out of her teens, with long blonde hair and a sequined red dress and matching heels. She looked a little drunk, like she'd been out partying and was now heading home.

Heading home. This would be her stop. She lived somewhere close.

And now she was walking right for him.

The screeching in his head made Brent wince in pain, like he had been hit by a sudden migraine.

Not now, he told himself. *You need to keep cool. Get to your storage unit and grab that bug-out bag and some other stuff. You can hunt later, when you're cleaned up and ready. Not now. Not now.*

The woman drew closer, eyeing Brent with no more than the usual suspicion.

Even though the metro station lay just ten meters ahead of him, Brent crossed the street. He'd walk until the girl went out of sight, then circle around and go take the metro.

Not now. Not now. Hunt tomorrow.

Out of the corner of his eye he saw the girl pass him on the opposite side of the street.

Not now. Not now. You got—ah, the hell with it.

He turned and stared at the girl. Yeah, strolling along without a care in the world. And no one else to see them.

Brent Richter waited until she turned a corner onto a side street before following, a smile on his face.

He wouldn't hear any screeching tonight. He'd sleep well, like he always did after gutting one of these bitches.

CHAPTER FIFTEEN

"Entschuldigung!"

Gillian Smith jerked and turned, startled at the sudden voice on the darkened street so late at night, then relaxed a little to see the man calling to her was on the other side of the street and a good ten feet down the road.

"Um, sorry. I don't speak German," she said, clutching her red scarf around her protectively.

The man waved his hand in the direction opposite from where Gillian was headed and spoke in broken English with a heavy accent.

"I … uh … find the Church of Saint Michael?"

"You mean you're looking for the Church of Saint Michael?" Gillian asked.

The handsome stranger snapped his fingers and smiled. "Ja. Looking for."

He held up his phone. "No data. I go to … how say?" he put his hands together in prayer and closed his eyes for a moment.

That put her even more at ease. A lost German looking to go to church while she stumbled home from a bender.

"Hold on," she said, pulling the phone out of her purse. "I think I saw it on the map. It's famous, right?"

"Yes. Famous," the stranger said, crossing the street but not angling toward her. Nice of him to leave her some space. Most guys didn't realize how scary it was for a woman to walk home alone at night.

The girl smiled. "Here it is."

She turned the phone to face him. Only then did he close the gap between them.

Gillian only felt a touch of nervousness as the stranger approached her. He was lost and polite, which put her at ease, and he didn't look like a creep. Plus they were standing less than half a block from a subway station.

Besides, she was on the University of Texas-Austin's woman's track and field team. If she kicked off these heels, she could outrun just about anybody. And this guy didn't look like the running type. More team sports and a good gym routine.

Yeah, well built, she thought, warming up to him. *Sure, I'll give you directions.*

As the stranger approached and Gillian got a better look at his face, she felt some disappointment. He looked older close up. Not *old* old, but too old for her.

"Danke schön. I not from here. I from Berlin," he said.

"I've been there! Crazy nightlife. Here's the church." Gillian held up her phone.

He studied it for a moment. "Oh, danke!"

"No problem. Enjoy your midnight mass."

The stranger nodded and took a couple of steps away before hesitating. "You want to come?"

Gillian's heart suddenly started beating hard. She took a step back.

"Uh? Oh, no. Thank you."

"The music is good."

"No, um, I'm kinda tired. Nice meeting you."

He shrugged.

"Auf Wiedersehen!" he said, and turned to walk away.

Gillian relaxed as she walked at a quick pace down the street, her high heels clacking on the pavement. At least this street wasn't cobblestone. She hated those. Normally she didn't wear heels at all, but this had been a formal party at the American Institute for the Erasmus students. The ambassador had even been there, for about half an hour before he left in his limo to something more important.

As she strolled away from the subway station, a lean figure walked toward her. He walked slouched, head hanging down with the visor of his baseball cap hiding his face. He wore one of those thin black leather jackets and black jeans. His sneakers were falling apart so much she could see the toe of his right sock.

Gillian bit her lip, clutched her purse a little tighter, and moved to the edge of the sidewalk. She decided if this guy gave her trouble she could always shout for that older guy. He'd come help. He was a bit weird the way he acted and how he tried to get her to go to church. Not really creepy, but so late at night? Still, he was probably a decent guy and she'd shout for him if she needed to.

The man in leather passed by and Gillian glanced over her shoulder to make sure he kept going. He did.

Good. She really didn't like walking home this late. At least she just had to take another left and go down the street a bit. Almost home.

After a few more steps she looked over her shoulder to check on the man in leather. He was still walking, still slouched, heading toward the subway station.

But why was that church guy still back there?

He stood close to the pool of light by the subway station, staring down at his phone.

Had he forgotten the directions she'd given him?

She almost stopped and called out to him, but felt embarrassed and kept walking.

Gillian turned the corner to get on her street. Other than a couple walking arm in arm way ahead of her, no one else was around. It didn't matter. Couples were safe and she was five minutes from home.

The couple turned and entered one of the houses. A reassuring light came on first downstairs, then upstairs as she continued forward. As she did, a strange, soft sound came to ears. A *wush wush wush wush* like a fan on in another room.

Except that it was growing louder.

Behind her!

She whirled, staggered a moment from the drink and the heels, and saw the churchgoer coming at her, taking a strange, wide stride that made his footfalls quieter. But even freakier was the guy's face. Even in the dim light she could see it was red, the features twisted, lips curled back in a snarl.

She was already running before she noticed his hands outstretched, fingers hook like claws, reaching.

Not running. Trying to run. She still had the damn heels on.

Gillian got to a streetlight, hoping vainly that its pool of radiance might protect her. The man rushed at her, no longer using that strange, sneaking gait, but instead sprinting straight for her, hands still extended.

She tore off one of her shoes, tossed it at the man, missed, and grabbed at the other.

Gillian wobbled as she pulled at it, grabbing at the streetlight to keep from falling down.

The man was almost at her. After a final tug, she got the shoe off, turned, and fled, letting out a scream.

Too late. She felt strong arms go around her middle. The man didn't slow down, but with immense strength lifted her off her feet and ran with her several steps to get to a shadowed doorway.

Gillian screamed again, screamed until he slammed her against the heavy wooden door and knocked the breath out of her. Then he let go of her waist …

… and clasped his strong hands around her neck.

Gillian lashed out, trying to knee him in the balls and only hitting his thigh. Her hands tried to pry off his grip, and found he was too strong. They struggled for a moment, Gillian's head throbbing, before she forced herself to let go and lash out at his face. She slammed a fist onto the side of his jaw, followed by raking the fingernails of her other hand across his face.

The man swore, and his grip loosened enough that Gillian was able to gulp some air for another scream. The plea for help got cut off as he drove a fist into her stomach. She doubled over, and if he hadn't been gripping her neck again she would have fallen.

Gillian felt herself get slammed against the wall again, a jolt of pain shooting through her head as her skull impacted with stone. She struggled, but could feel herself growing weak, uncoordinated.

This is how I die. Why? Why do I have to die like this?

Her life didn't flash before her eyes like everyone says it does. No, instead she only saw one thing, the only thing, she realized, that actually mattered.

Her family. Mom and Dad and her little brother Tyler who she always complained about being annoying but who she had bought a big book on European castles for his birthday. She saw them, and they were smiling at her, loving her as much as she loved them despite the petty bickering and little misunderstandings that filled any family life. Despite the distance she had put between them by going to college out of state, and then moving even further away to Europe on the Erasmus program. Despite the fact that she only Facetimed with them once or twice a week since she went to college. Despite the fact that she thought about her friends at college and the guys she like more than them.

Despite all that, at this last moment, they were the ones who she saw.

She clung on to their image. As the rest of the world faded, she focused only on them. If this was really happening, if this really was where it all ended, then she wanted her last connection to be with them.

Her lungs heaved, flooding themselves with sweet air. She hadn't even felt the attacker's hands let go but her body reacted automatically. Another breath, more gulping for air, and her vision cleared enough to see that she had fallen to her knees, one hand flat on the ground to support her.

Relief mingled with a new fear.

What if he doesn't want to kill me? What if he wants to ...

A scuffle nearby made her look up. Her attacker was grappling with another guy. It took Gillian a moment to realize it was that slim man in the leather jacket she had been nervous about earlier. And coming up the street was a middle-aged man. He looked like a construction worker with a big belly and hefty arms.

The man in the leather jacket clung onto her attacker as the two traded punches. The attacker was obviously winning, but the man in the leather jacket didn't give up, hunching his shoulders against the punches as he flailed back at him.

With a final push, the man who had tried to strangle Gillian tore away from his opponent's grip and bolted. The middle aged man chased after him, but the attacker sprinted up the street, soon leaving the older man huffing and puffing far behind.

The man in the leather jacket came up to Gillian.

"Are you all right?"

Gillian didn't reply. She remained on her knees, shivering and crying.

No, she wasn't all right. She wouldn't be all right for a long, long time.

CHAPTER SIXTEEN

Alexa watched Dieter Weiss sitting in handcuffs in front of a police sergeant's desk at the Munich central police station as the sergeant processed him, and thought about how stupid some civilians could be. His first reaction back at the Richters' country estate had been to flee, when all he needed to do was give himself up peacefully and answer a few questions.

Maybe he's not stupid. Maybe he has something to hide, Alexa thought. Astrid had grilled him about the murders, but he seemed genuinely shocked and unaware they had occurred. So if he really was hiding something, it was something else.

Probably drugs, Alexa thought, *or cheating with a married woman. It's usually one of the two.*

So many civilian thought they were being rebellious individuals when really all they were doing were the same old crimes Alexa had seen a million times before.

Alexa yawned. It was getting late, and she needed some sleep. They'd have to start fresh the next morning. It looked like Brent Richter was laying low for a while now that he had managed to get to Germany.

Stuart came up to her, phone in hand.

"Any news from the States?" she asked.

"Nothing from the higher-ups, but I did get something from Stacy."

Alexa perked up. Stuart held up his phone. Alexa saw a series of photos of herself feeding that horse by the side of the road.

Beneath that was a reply from Stacy of a smiling emoji with hearts for eyes.

"That's it?" Alexa asked, feeling disappointed.

"You know the old saying. 'An emoji is worth a thousand words.'"

"Isn't that 'a picture is worth a thousand words'?"

Stuart grinned. "Get with the times."

Alexa checked her phone. Nothing from Stacy.

She sent him a message and not me?

Her feelings must have been apparent on her face because Stuart said, "Don't worry. She's still sulking but she's getting over it. She replied to photos with you in them."

"She replied to photos of the horse."

"No, she replied to photos of you feeding the horse. That means she replied to something involving you. She's acknowledging you. Indirectly. Because she wants to show she's still mad at you. It's communication, which is better than what you had before."

"Since when were you a psychologist?"

"Since I joined the Behavioral Affairs Unit."

"I didn't know they taught courses on sulky teenagers."

"Serial killers? Sulky teenagers? Is it really that much of a leap?"

Astrid hurried up to them. "Stop staring at your phones and follow me. There's been another attack, right here in Munich! A blonde woman attacked by a lone male. She was wearing red. Some passersby chased him away. Their descriptions sound like Richter. My colleagues are at the scene now."

Alexa was so shocked she didn't even have time to feel annoyed about that comment about the phones.

* * *

The attack had occurred in Munich's historic center, and Astrid shot the police car through narrow, winding lanes past imposing public buildings, through cobblestone squares, and beneath the soaring spires of Gothic cathedrals.

Alexa had eyes for none of this beauty. Richter was close, and every second it took to get to the crime scene, the more time he had to get away.

He'd already proven he didn't need much of a chance to give them the slip.

Astrid spun around a corner, the side of the car scraping against a stone wall, and pulled to a stop near a subway station. Nearby another police car and an ambulance were parked. Alexa could see an officer interviewing a young man in a leather jacket and an older man with a beer belly.

They hopped out and rushed over. Astrid got there first and began to talk to them in German. Frustrated at being left out of the conversation, Alexa walked over to the ambulance.

Inside she saw the old familiar scene—a victim getting the professional care of a team of EMTs, medics trained to help with whatever physical injuries the victim might have, but incapable of healing the deep hurt in the victim's soul from being the target of random violence.

Alexa saw a young woman of about twenty, sitting slumped in the ambulance as a female EMT checked her blood pressure. The woman had a neck brace on, and Alexa could see severe bruises all around the neck.

That's from strangling, Alexa realized, having seen marks like that way too often. *He tried to strangle her. Why did he change his technique?*

Then Alexa got another surprise—the victim wasn't wearing red. Her dress was yellow. No red shoes, no red handbag.

Then she saw a gauzy red scarf lying on the seat next to her.

In a quiet voice, Alexa asked, "Excuse me, do you speak English?"

The woman—more a girl, really—moved her entire body to face her since she couldn't turn her neck.

"Y-yes. Who are you?"

The victim had a Texas accent.

Probably doing a year abroad, the high point of her life, and this happens.

"I'm Deputy U.S. Marshal Alexa Chase."

The girl blinked. "U.S. Marshal?"

"My partner and I are in Germany hunting a serial killer who fled from the United States."

"An American?"

"German American."

The victim's eyes widened. "He pretended he didn't speak good English! He asked for directions to some church and then followed me. If it wasn't for those two guys, I would have … I would have … "

The woman shook all over.

"Is that your scarf?" Alexa asked.

"My scarf? Um, yeah."

"Were you wearing it when you were attacked?"

"Yeah."

It's always been red dresses before. Is a red scarf enough? Did having the triggering color around the neck make him decide to change his M.O.? does that mean there are more murders than we thought?

Alexa looked around the darkened streets, as if they would give her an answer.

He's close. But where?

Stuart stood talking with Astrid, and nearby an officer hunched over the open door of his patrol car, speaking on the radio.

I bet they're setting up a cordon. Good luck with that on these twisty little streets.

Good luck with that and this perp.

More as a matter of routine, she pulled out the folded up printouts of the police sketches and showed them to the victim.

"Is this the man who attacked you?"

The woman stared at them a moment.

"I think so."

"You think so?"

"Well, he didn't quite look like this. And it says here he's six-two. He was maybe five ten. I'm five nine and he was barely taller than me. Strong, though. So strong … "

The woman shivered. Alexa grimaced, shuffling through the printouts. They all looked subtly different, and the estimated heights and weights were all over the place. No wonder this poor kid couldn't make a positive ID.

"Have you already made a statement to the local police?"

"Yeah. Those guys that helped me are doing that too."

"Thank you. One of the officers will see you home."

Alexa moved back toward Astrid and the two witnesses when the officer talking on the radio shouted something. There was a great babble of German and Astrid ran for her patrol car. On instinct, Alexa and Stuart ran after her.

CHAPTER SEVENTEEN

They got the story only after Astrid had popped into gear and driven a block down the road. Alexa fumbled for her seatbelt. This woman was almost as crazy a driver as Stuart. Alexa wondered if she was a veteran who used to drive through hostile fire too. She didn't know if the Germans sent anyone to Iraq, but if they did, Astrid would be a good recruit.

"A woman just called the emergency number not one minute ago," Astrid said. "Some blonde man tried to strangle her. It's not far."

A minute. Alexa fidgeted. You can move pretty far in a minute. Take three or four turns on these old streets. Maybe get on a subway or a bus if you're lucky. Or hop into a car. She wouldn't be surprised if Richter had a car in storage, waiting for his return to Munich.

Damn. We could have lost him already.

Astrid screeched to a halt in a small, circular plaza, nearly colliding with a splashing stone fountain in the center. They got out, and found the night silent. All the cafes were shut, their chairs and tables piled up and secured with chains, their doors shut tight. Only a few lights shone from the upper story apartments. No one was in sight.

"This way," Astrid said. "My colleague is going around to get behind the suspect's last location."

"Does he have backup?"

"He'll be fine."

Alexa wondered about that. She'd heard that line far too often, and things hadn't always turned out so good.

As if reading her thoughts, Astrid added, "More units are coming to the area."

Alexa cocked her ear and didn't hear sirens. Good. Astrid hadn't put hers on either. The local cops knew when to be cautious.

Astrid led them down one of the five narrow cobblestone lanes that converged on this plaza. Alexa wondered how she could tell them apart. All the streets around here looked the same.

"He could have run two main directions," Astrid huffed as she ran along. "My colleague is guarding one way. This is the other."

A figure in a hooded sweatshirt strolled down the lane toward them, hands in his or her pockets.

"Halt!" Astrid shouted, pulling her nightstick and running up to him.

She got within a few paces of him and stopped short. A moment later Alexa, running just behind, saw why. The man looked like a Turk. Or perhaps Syrian. Wherever he was from, she doubted there was much blonde hair in his family.

A quick question from Astrid, a shrug from the Turk, and they ran on.

"He didn't see anything," Astrid grumbled. "They never see anything."

What's that supposed to mean?

A bit further on, they came to a fork in the road. Tall, gabled buildings hemmed them in on all sides. Beside the narrow sidewalk was a solid column of parked cars. Far along one lane, three older woman walked side by side. Alexa squinted. She didn't see any red on them.

"We split up," Astrid said. "Stuart, follow those women. Alexis, we go the other way."

"Alexa," Alexa corrected, but Astrid was already running down the road.

Alexa kept a nervous eye on those vehicles. Richter could hide under the bigger Jeeps and vans, or simply duck behind a smaller car if he saw them coming.

They passed a group of drunk teenagers, who said something obscene when Astrid asked them a question, and then came to another plaza, a bigger one this time lined with imposing old stone buildings. Like in the other plaza, this one had stacks of chairs and tables all around it from the closed cafes, although one bar at the far end still had lights and music filtering out of an open front door. A few teenagers sat on the steps of an old monument with a statue of some man Alexa didn't recognize, drinking cans of beer and staring at Astrid.

She and Alexa stopped for a second, looking around. There was only one other way out, which after a short stretch led to a busy, well-lit road.

"We have already positioned officers on that road," Astrid said, pointing.

“So either he slipped past us or he’s in Stuart’s direction,” Alexa replied.

Just as they turned to go back the way they came, Alexa spotted movement out of the corner of her eye. She looked toward a stack of tables on the far side of the plaza, where the light was dim and no one stood around. She stopped and stared. Nothing.

“What?” Astrid asked.

“I thought I saw something. Now I’m not so sure.”

By unspoken consensus they walked toward the stack of tables. There was clear space for a good ten feet to either side until to the right there was another stack of tables from an adjoining café, and to the left stretched a long row of recycling bins set so closely there was no space between them. Alexa tried to see everything at the same time.

“Keep your eyes unfocused,” Powers always used to tell her. “Don’t look at any particular thing, just keep your eyes set at the middle of the field you’re looking at. They’ll pick up anything strange and point that way automatically. Try to look too hard and you’re liable to miss something.”

She’d found that advice really worked, although it was hard to follow in the dark in an unfamiliar city. Her gaze kept darting around, especially since she wasn’t sure she had really seen anything there.

Alexa took a deep breath and tried to relax her eyes. Just as she did, they turned toward the stack again. Had something moved at the edge of it?

Alexa turned her head a bit to the side, as if she was looking at something else. That made Astrid turn too.

But it was a trick, Alexa kept her eyes focused on that stack, hoping in the dim light whoever was behind it couldn’t see where her eyes pointed, only the direction of her face.

A blonde, well-built man darted out from behind the stack, heading for the bins.

Got you!

Alexa sprinted for him, smiling. The guy thought he might make it, and without that trick he might have. He ran with a strange gait that ate up the ground but also didn’t make a sound.

It didn’t matter. He wasn’t getting away.

“Halt!” Astrid shouted, waving her nightstick. The man jerked and disappeared behind the bins.

Alexa didn't have a stick, only a gun and some pepper spray. The suspect didn't seem armed and so she wasn't sure what German law allowed her to do.

She yanked out the pepper spray.

Astrid angled to the left to go around the far end of the bins. Alexa kept straight on, rounding the near corner of the bins where the man had disappeared.

She guessed right. He leapt around the corner, thinking both would try to head him off and he could gain a lead by retracing his steps, but instead he nearly bumped into a Deputy U.S. Marshal.

Richter stopped, backpedaled, and got a cloud of pepper spray straight in the face.

He coughed, waving his hands in front of his face in a fruitless attempt to clear the air. Then he spun around to run.

In his shock, Richter lost his bearings and ran straight into the bins. The impact of his face into the big plastic containers made a satisfying thud, as did the sound of his body falling to the pavement.

Alexa put away her pepper spray, pulled out a pair of handcuffs, and tried to flip him over.

Richter still had some fight in him, though, and lashed out at her. Half blind, his body wracked with coughs, he only managed to punch her shoulder. Alexa grabbed his arm, put it in an armlock, and used her leverage to twist him until he ended up face down on the pavement. Then she put a knee to the small of his back and cuffed him.

A sound to her left made her look. Astrid had come running up, nightstick in hand, looking a bit disappointed.

"You have to leave some for the international visitors," Alexa said with a smile.

Alexa hauled Richter to his feet. Now that the adrenaline was beginning to wear off, she noticed his clothes were damp in places, and there was the sharp smell of fresh urine.

"Ugh, I think he peed himself."

"No," Astrid said, pointing. "He fell in a puddle, and both of you rolled around in it."

With a sense of dread, Alexa looked down. The German police officer was right. A big damp stain took up the space beneath their feet, and similar stains were all over her uniform and Richter's clothing.

"Here you are," Astrid said, handing her a tissue.

"That's not going to cut it."

"Cut it?" Astrid said, her English faltering for the first time.

Richter shouted something in German, struggling in his handcuffs.

"We need to wash his eyes," Astrid said. "Let's go to that bar and get some water."

As they walked over, Astrid spoke to the prisoner. Alexa assumed he was reading him his rights. A laugh from the teens hanging out at the monument told her where the piss had probably come from.

I wonder if I can arrest them for soiling an officer of the law, Alexa thought.

Despite feeling disgusting, her mood was buoyant. They had nabbed Richter in less than 24 hours of getting to Germany.

"You led us on a hell of a chase," Alexa told him.

"Was?" Richter tried to stare at her through his puffy, tearing eyes.

"Don't pretend you don't understand me."

Richter turned and said something to Astrid. A quick conversation followed. Astrid cursed and fished into his pocket, pulling out a wallet.

The name on the identity card was not Brent Richter.

"It must be fake," Alexa protested.

Astrid searched the other pockets but did not find a knife.

"We'll see," the German officer said. "Stay here with him and I'll get some water from the bar."

Astrid ducked inside. A few old men with bellies like beer kegs gathered at the doorway to stare at the two stained and smelly people, one a German with bloodshot eyes, the other some foreign woman in an unfamiliar uniform.

"Where did you get the fake ID?" Alexa asked the prisoner.

"Ich spreche kein Englisch."

"Cut the crap."

"Leck mich am Arsch!"

The fat old drinkers chuckled.

"You want a translation?" one of them offered.

"No, thank you. I think I have a pretty good idea."

Astrid returned with a dirty dishcloth and a beer mug full of water and began cleaning his eyes.

As she did, Alexa took a closer look at the prisoner in the light of the bar. The victim was right, he was shorter than the American witnesses said, and his hair was longer. Plus his features were thinner, and his body thicker, more muscular and stout.

Alexa got a sinking feeling.

But it must be him!

A police car pulled up and two officers got out. One of them gave the prisoner a sarcastically jovial greeting. Astrid asked the officer something and there was a brief exchange. Astrid slumped.

Oh, crap.

She turned to Alexa and told her what she had been dreading to hear.

"My colleague recognizes him. He's been arrested twice for beating his wife. The identity card is real. This is not Brent Richter."

Another policeman arrived with a thin man in a black leather jacket. The civilian pointed to the suspect and started speaking in German. Astrid slumped a little further.

"He just confirmed this was the man who attacked the American with the red scarf. Just a random crime. This has nothing to do with Richter."

Alexa winced. *And the trail just keeps getting colder.*

CHAPTER EIGHTEEN

Alexa's phone tore her out of a deep sleep. She fumbled for it in the darkness of her hotel room as her mind tried to piece together her situation. After processing the suspect at the station, Astrid had driven them to their hotel so they could crash and start fresh in the morning.

But the clock on the bedside table said 6:05 am. Not her idea of starting fresh. Stuart wouldn't be calling her at this hour.

She turned on her phone. "Stacy?"

"Do I look like a thirteen-year-old girl to you?" Stuart asked.

"Oh. Sorry. I'm half asleep."

"I'm three-quarters asleep. We'll grab some coffee on the way to the airport."

"Airport?"

"Astrid just called. There's been another murder. A blonde woman in a red dress. In France."

Alexa stumbled out of bed, groping for the light.

"France?"

"Yeah, Paris. Astrid has booked us an early flight. She's coming too. She's picking us up in half an hour. Your uniform still smell of piss?"

"The hotel laundered it."

"Wish I had a laundry service in Iraq. Ever have to hit the dirt under fire and realize you've landed in a pile of camel turds?"

"No."

"It ain't pretty. Let's get going."

* * *

The crime scene wasn't pretty either. Four hours later, they stood on a back street with a pair of French gendarmes, looking at a chalk outline of a body in the center of a huge pool of dried blood.

That's all they had managed to see, though. The gendarmes were far from happy to have officers from two foreign nations showing up uninvited to their murder investigation. They hadn't shared any details and hadn't even showed them the crime scene photos Alexa could see poking out from a folder in one of the gendarme's hands.

"This is an American citizen who were are pursuing in Europe," Stuart explained for the tenth time. "We have permission from Interpol, my government, and the European Union."

Alexa looked around. A narrow street that turned in both directions so this straight portion measured barely a hundred yards long. Late at night, Richter could have caught her and killed her without much chance of being spotted.

But didn't he want to run a risk? Wasn't that how he got off? Perhaps doing it in the center of town was risky enough. Or maybe he was losing control, unable to curb his urges long enough to set it up the way he liked it. She'd read about serial killers that escalated so much that they ended up getting sloppy.

That helped the police catch them, but not before they left a trail of dead bodies in their wake.

And how to catch him? He moves so fast. Once he got off that plane to Munich, he must have bolted for the border, figuring the first place we'd search for him would be Germany.

She turned back to the argument, which didn't seem to have progressed at all. Stuart and Astrid kept showing their authorization, and the two gendarmes kept clicking their tongues and shaking their heads.

Alexa snorted. She hated it when different agencies started having their little territorial spats. It had been even worse on the Drake Logan manhunt, with everyone from the FBI to Border Patrol tearing up the countryside looking for him and not sharing their information. Each unit wanted to be the one to claim the prize. In the end, it had been Alexa and Stuart together. She'd heard comments from other U.S. Marshals complaining that the FBI had "stolen half our glory."

Stuart hadn't stolen a damn thing. She probably wouldn't have caught Logan without his help. Or would have died trying.

Sensing that the argument wasn't going to end anytime soon, Alexa wandered off to look at the neighborhood.

"Walk around," Powers always said. "Take a look at the area. Criminals commit crimes in places where they feel comfortable. That counts double for career criminals, and triple for serial killers. Those nut jobs are obsessed with getting everything just right."

Nut jobs. He liked that word. Used it for a lot of criminal types. Except that he walked around for several days with a straight razor fantasizing about slashing people's faces.

That was to get into a psychopath's head. He wouldn't have ever done it. He just went too far trying to understand the criminal mind, like you've gone too far.

Too many times.

Alexa shoved those painful thoughts away and paid attention to the streets around her.

The neighborhood appeared mostly residential, with a few small shops and cafes serving the local residents. This was one of the oldest parts of Paris, Astrid had told her, with lots of winding little streets dating back centuries. Little alleys led to small courtyards. Road converged at plazas like spokes on a wheel. The turns on the streets made it so that you could never see more than a couple of hundred yards ahead, and usually a lot less.

This neighborhood was public, but offered plenty of places to hide, plenty of places to run.

He wants to risk it, but not risk it too much. He's resourceful, though, and intelligent. He must realize he's going to get caught eventually. Maybe that's why he's escalating, to up the body count before the inevitable.

Alexa turned a corner and stopped short. On the side of a building taller than its neighbor hung a billboard advertising some sort of cabaret. It featured three female dancers, the one featured in the center a lovely young blonde in a red, low-cut gown. In large letters beneath her it said, "Mademoiselle Dubois."

Just beyond, she saw an entrance to a Paris Metro station.

This would have been the most logical way to leave. Hop on the Metro and get anywhere he wants. If he came this way, he would definitely have seen that cabaret ad.

Alexa pulled out a phone and took a photo of the billboard, then hurried back to where her partner and the others still stood arguing next to the crime scene. Obviously the argument hadn't gotten anywhere. The photos remained in the gendarme's folder.

It didn't matter. She knew where Richter would strike next.

"Look!" she shouted as she held up her phone.

"Whoa," Stuart said. "Where did you see that?"

"Just up the road there, right next to the nearest Metro station."

“He probably saw that,” Astrid said.

Stuart nodded. “Yeah, and he’s not going to be able to resist.”

They turned to the two gendarmes. Only one of them spoke English.

“We need to get some plainclothes officers posted there as soon as it opens,” Alexa said.

“You say this murderer kills yellow-haired women who wear red?” the gendarme asked.

“Yes.”

He waved his hand in a dismissive gesture. “Then it could be any woman.”

“But the sign is so close to the murder location.”

“He might have gone that way, or he might not. Your reasoning is thin.”

Your professionalism is thin.

Alexa gathered her patience and replied, “Is this a common advertisement?”

“Yes, I have seen several sign boards for this cabaret in central Paris.”

“You see?” Stuart said. “Even more of a chance he’s spotted one. He likes risk. He’ll want to kill someone who’s a public figure.”

The gendarme shrugged. “We don’t even know if this is your crazy American … ” he turned to Astrid. “ … or does Germany claim him?”

Astrid glowered at him. The gendarme ignored her and went on. “We have stabbings like this all too often. A red dress proves nothing. We will investigate, and of course we will call the cabaret and tell them to be on their guard, but we cannot afford to put a plainclothesman there all night for as long as this man is at large.”

“But—”

Alexa got cut off. “You have to understand that we are overloaded, as I’m sure your department is. We have stabbings all the time, and burglaries, and the Turkish and Syrian gangs have started a war. We don’t have the resources for this.”

“I’m sure this is the work by the same man,” Alexa said. “Could I at least see the crime scene photos?”

The second gendarme, who was carrying the folder, suddenly clutched it tighter.

Turns out you do know English, eh?

“I’m afraid that’s impossible. I don’t have authorization from my superiors. If you apply at the central precinct perhaps you can convince them.”

And how long will that take? Alexa fumed. *More time than we have. Fine. You can investigate like this is an isolated incident. The three of us can handle Richter.*

I sure hope he shows up where he’s supposed to, instead of going off after a different blonde in a red dress.

CHAPTER NINETEEN

Brent Richter had never liked the cabaret. All that fake happiness and showing off reminded him of sex. But he sure wanted to go to the Montparnasse Follies. Puzzling through the French on the website, he discovered it offered a "night of decadence, laughs, and old Parisian splendor." Sounded like a tourist trap, except the website was only in French. Maybe it was for French tourists from the provinces. The Parisians could be snooty about people from other parts of France.

Or people from anywhere other than Paris.

Perhaps I should speak to them in German just to annoy them, he thought with a smile as he got off the Metro. *No, better to act like a clueless American tourist, annoy them with my mediocre French, and get backstage somehow. Flash some money. That works everywhere. Hans taught me that.*

The Montparnasse Follies stood on a two-lane street with a fair amount of traffic as well as several shops and cafes that remained open even though it was already past ten. Brent felt his skin prickle and his breath come more rapidly as he saw all the people, all the potential witnesses. This was going to be tough. This was going to be *fun.*

The façade of the cabaret was of fake oak beams and whitewashed walls like some quaint structure from the nineteenth century. An old-style gas lamp hung above the door, its flickering light shining through red panes. The doorman was a huge West African in a top hat and greatcoat. Brent reminded himself to keep an eye on him. A switchblade wouldn't stop this guy fast enough to keep him from popping Brent's head off his shoulders like a champagne cork.

He'd charm him instead.

Brent cracked a grin. "Bonjour, mon ami!"

The bouncer nodded politely but didn't respond. Brent shook his hand, slipping him a twenty-euro note.

"I'm sorry I don't know much French. Do you speak English?"

"I do," the man said in a deep baritone.

"Ah, good. Are there still seats? Something up front."

“Certainly, sir. Let’s step inside and I’ll have a word with the ticket seller.”

Brent smiled again. *Yes, you know that twenty wasn’t for the ticket, do you?*

The bouncer opened the door for him, they entered, and Brent froze just beyond the threshold.

What he saw there almost made him convulse. They stood in a short entrance hallway, the other end veiled by a red satin curtain. Through the small window of the ticket booth to his right he saw a middle-aged woman.

Blonde. In a dress that matched the red satin of the curtain.

Control yourself. You want the dancer, not her.

Maybe I can get both. Oh, wouldn’t that be perfect!

Clearing his throat and clenching his fists to control the shaking of his hands, Brent stepped up to the ticket window. The bouncer said something in French. Brent caught the word “special”. Yes, a special guest who gave good tips. The woman smiled and said, “Tickets are thirty euros, and we have a good table right up front.”

“Thank you.” He handed over a fifty euro note. “Keep the change.”

I’ll get it back later.

The bouncer gave a little bow and gestured to the red satin curtain. Brent passed through.

Once again he was nearly overcome with shaking as the soft red material pressed against his face and body.

“You know I love you,” his mother used to coo at him when he was little, pressing him against the red dresses that she loved to wear. “I’m sorry I shout sometimes, and I’m sorry that I hit you.” He’d hug her closer. Maybe this time she meant it. Maybe this time everything would be all right.

“I love you so much,” she’d say again. “That’s why I’m strict with you, so you’ll grow up right.”

Gaslighting. Even before he knew the word he knew all about it. But when you’re six or eight or ten, you want to think it’s true this time, that everything would be better, while deep in your heart you know it’s all a lie, and that the hitting will start soon enough. And the lies. And the mockery.

Brent Richter shuddered as he passed through the curtain and stumbled into the cabaret.

And nearly had a heart attack.

All the waitstaff were women, and they all wore identical red silk dresses.

Jesus Christ! How the hell am I going to keep it together! At least none of them are blondes. Oh, crap, the bartender is.

A waitress came up to him and asked him something he didn't hear, and wouldn't have understood even if she had spoken in English or German. His mind was a whirlwind of emotions and bloody fantasies. Dumbly he handed over his ticket, she smiled and said something else, the words coming out muffled as if she spoke from underneath the water. As if in a dream he followed her, bumping once against a table because all he had eyes for were those red dresses.

At last he found himself sitting at a table right next to the stage. He choked out a drink order and the waitress left.

Brent closed his eyes for a moment, making a supreme effort to get himself under control. He had visions of leaping over the bar, stabbing that blonde bartender in the gut enough for her to bleed out, then tearing through the rest of the waitstaff before breaking into the ticket booth and giving that ticket seller a good twenty in the stomach.

He half rose from his chair before forcing himself to sit down.

No. Get the star. Get the one everyone knows from the posters. That will be the bigger hit. And if you have a chance, get some of the others as well.

Taking a deep breath, Brent opened his eyes. He focused on the empty stage with its red silk curtains (*damn it!*) and ignored the waitstaff he could hear moving around him.

He checked his watch. The show didn't start for another twenty minutes. Could he last out here another twenty minutes?

Brent was ninety percent sure he couldn't.

What to do? He looked around, taking in the room for the first time, forcing his eyes to pass over the women in red silk to focus on where he had landed himself.

The room was fairly large, with about thirty tables, more than half of them full and more people coming in. Not bad for a weekday. This place must be pretty popular. A bar ran along the righthand wall, but Brent quickly looked away from that to avoid lingering on that bartender who really needed to have her intestines rearranged.

There wasn't much else to see, just old paintings of dancers and nude women on the walls, and a fake nineteenth-century décor of gilt and gas lamps.

Other than where he had come in, he saw two doors. One stood to the left of stage and had a sign in green and red stating, "Sortie de secours, à n'utiliser qu'en cas d'urgence." He figured that was the emergency exit. Good to know. He'd already scouted the area a few hours ago and knew it led to the street behind. But the depth of this room and stage weren't as much as the depth of the building, so there must be a hallway beyond that door before getting to the actual back door.

Which meant that behind the stage there was more space. Of course, for the dressing rooms and prop room.

And how to get there? By a door to the right of the stage, marked by a sign saying, "Employés seulement."

Employees only. Perfect. He could slip in there, find the star's dressing room, gut her like a fish, and then return to do the bartender before running out the emergency exit.

He'd miss the ticket seller, but if he managed to get away, he could take out one or two more people before he police finally ran him down. Especially if he could make it to Brussels, where he had another storage locker. There was a Eurostar overnight train that could get him there.

All right. Now he had a plan. Two for one. Great. But how the hell could he get through that door?

Money. That usually worked. His father had spent a lifetime accruing it, only to have his wife and children waste it. What a pushover that guy had been. Married to his mother all those years and never once slapped her. Never even had the backbone to get a divorce.

Probably because he liked picking on Brent too much. The youngest. The most vulnerable in the family besides his own worthless self. His father hadn't been as bad as his screeching mother, but he did join in, acting like a simpering sidekick to his wife. God he wished he gave that guy a few stabs before cancer took him! His mother too. If only he had developed the willpower before she had that stroke.

Brent shook himself. He needed to get out of the past and into the present. He had things to do, and a waitress coming up to his table provided him the opportunity.

"Do you speak English?" he asked.

"A little. Yes." She smiled at him. Such a fake smile, just like the décor was fake, and the entire concept of a cabaret was fake. At least she wasn't a blonde. He could talk to her without his voice cracking.

"Do you sell roses?" These places usually did.

"Flowers? Oh yes!"

"Could you send a dozen roses to Mademoiselle Dubois?" He handed her a hundred euro note. "Keep the change. And bring the roses to me for a moment, will you?"

The waitress smiled, eyes glittering at the generous tip, and hurried off. Within a minute she was back with a bouquet of a dozen roses.

He had anticipated he might have to take this route, and so he was ready. He stuck another hundred euro note in with the roses, then added a business card he had printed up just a couple of hours before. It read, "Brent Richter, Talent Scout, Hollywood" and gave a fake email and phone number.

Brent figured this could go one of several ways. A lot of these places fronted for prostitution. He didn't think one advertised as much as the Montparnasse Follies would be, but that hundred euro note would reveal it. Or perhaps she wanted a sugar daddy. Either way it would get him back stage. Or maybe she'd fall for the talent scout line if she was dumb enough. He'd mainly put that in there as an excuse, a cover so people could ignore the obvious hint of the hundred euros.

Or she could take the roses, take the money, and ignore him.

If that happened, he'd choose the nuclear option and stab her on stage. That man mountain guarding the door would barrel in and Brent would have to escape without killing anyone else, but at least he'd get the dancer.

Brent fidgeted as the waitress disappeared through the employees only door. She came out just a minute later and walked up to him with a smile.

"Mademoiselle Dubois would be happy to meet you after the show."

I can't hold back that long. Should I just kill her on stage? But then I don't get a chance at that bartender.

I got to do it now. Just walk through that door if I have to.

No. If I do that, they'll call the bouncer. I can't take him. Damn it!

"Monsieur?"

The waitress looked concerned. Brent thought fast.

"Oh, it's just that it's a terrible disappointment. You see, I have to have a late business dinner with a French director right after the show. Frans Bernard. Do you know him?"

The waitress's eyes lit up. "But of course! He is a great artist."

"Could I just have a quick word with her before I go? Just one minute. Then I'll see the show and I'll really have to get going."

He looked at his Rolex to emphasize his hurry, and to emphasize his wealth.

The waitress smiled. "I am sure Mademoiselle Dubois could give you just one minute."

"That would be wonderful. Thank you."

They moved to the door, Brent's heart beating fast. He put a hand in his pocket and grasped his switchblade.

OK. This chick is probably going to stay so she can escort me out. Cut her throat to get rid of her. That way you can spend a bit more time on Mademoiselle Dubois. Stab her good. If you've managed to do all that without one of them screaming for help, rush out and get the bartender. Just rush out as fast as you can, jump over the bar, and give it to her before anyone knows what's happening.

They passed through the door and entered a short hallway with several doors on the righthand wall, the one opposite the stage. The first stood open, and Brent recognized one of the other dancers from the billboard in there, putting on makeup while chatting to a man in a black suit. Brent barely noticed either of them, or the woman in regular clothes standing at the end of the hallway checking her phone. Probably a manager or something. It didn't matter. He had thoughts for only one thing.

They came to the next door, which was closed. The waitress knocked, got a soft reply, and opened up.

She sat at the dressing table with her back to him, already wearing her red gown. It didn't seem to fit right, though, and her blonde hair was cut short. Did she usually wear a wig? She held up a tiara in front of her, and so he couldn't see her face in the reflection of her mirror.

He paused, waiting for the waitress to leave. To his surprise, she rushed out of the room.

Brent cleared his throat, reaching his hand into his pocket.

"Bonjour, Mademoiselle Dubois."

The woman dropped the tiara, reached under a cloth on the table in front of her, and stood.

When she whipped around, Brent saw two things.

One, this wasn't Mademoiselle Dubois.

Two, she had pulled out a police officer's nightstick.

"Brent Richter," she shouted in German, "you are—"

Brent didn't wait for the rest. He leapt back, yanking the switchblade out of his pocket. A moment later the nightstick whooshed just an inch past his face. He kept backpedaling.

Until he hit a hard body behind him.

Strong hands grasped his knife arm. Brent elbowed the other man in the ribs. His unseen assailant let out a grunt and kneed him in the back of the legs.

It was meant to make him fall, but Brent only stumbled forward, crashing into the dressing table along with his attacker. He looked over his shoulder and saw it was the man in the suit from the other dressing room. The woman from the hallway hand entered the dressing room too.

"FBI! Quit resisting!" the man in the suit shouted. This was emphasized by him smashing Brent's knife hand into the mirror, shattering the glass. Pain lanced through his hand and he dropped the knife.

Roaring with rage, he tried to tear out of the FBI's man's grasp. They spun around, Brent freeing one arm, ready to punch, when the woman from the hallway stepped forward and gave him a right cross that left his head spinning.

The next thing he knew he was being slammed face first onto the carpet. The FBI man's knee pressed hard against his back. He heard the rattle of metal and felt the handcuffs clamp around his wrists.

Brent Richter relaxed, then began to chuckle.

"Did pretty good. There won't be any screeching in my cell. No, no screeching at all. I'll finally have some peace."

CHAPTER TWENTY

Mademoiselle Dubois needed a hot bath, a cigarette, and at least half a bottle of wine. When those foreign officers came to the cabaret and told her that her life was in danger, at first she didn't believe it, but then the gendarmerie called her manager, saying that a blonde woman in a red dress had been killed, and that an American serial killer targeting women of that description had fled to Europe.

So she agreed to give the German officer her dress and let her act as bait. Mademoiselle Dubois hid in her manager's office with the door locked.

She heard later that the officers nearly had a heart attack when they saw Beatrice take up her position at the bar. No one had thought to mention to them that Beatrice was a blonde. Well, a bottle blonde, but still blonde enough to be in danger. By then then, the killer was already entering. Vivienne was at her post in the ticket booth. The officers had allowed that, as long as she kept the door locked and Luis, the Spanish assistant bouncer, hiding under her desk.

All trained actresses, the ladies of the Montparnasse Follies had played their roles perfectly.

Mademoiselle Dubois shuddered. Every few minutes, the reality of what had just occurred would overcome her.

"Are you all right?" asked Eloise, one of the other waitresses who offered to take her home. They walked arm in arm through her neighborhood.

"I can't believe that happened only an hour ago. I feel like I'm still living it."

Eloise gave her hand a squeeze. "You're safe now. You should have seen him as they dragged him out. They really worked him over. Your dressing room is a mess, I'm afraid."

"Ugh. Monsieur Duplantier will try to find a way to take it out of my salary. You know how he is."

"At least everyone gets the night off."

Even though Monsieur Duplantier was notoriously tight-fisted, even he wouldn't think of having a show after a bloody American serial killer had been dragged through the bar area in front of the entire audience.

"He'll probably take that out of our wages too," Mademoiselle Dubois grumbled.

Eloise laughed. "I can see you're feeling better, if you're able to complain about that old cheapskate!"

"Here we are. Thank you so much for walking me home. I know I'm being silly, with him already under arrest, but—"

"Don't be ridiculous! Of course you needed someone to walk you home. You want me to come up?"

"No, that's all right. You have to get home to your father. How is he, by the way?"

"About the same," Eloise said with a sigh. "The doctors say he might never improve."

Mademoiselle Dubois gave Eloise a kiss on both cheeks.

"You sure you'll be all right?" Eloise asked.

"Yes. I'm much better now. And my sister is coming over in an hour to spend the evening with me."

"All right," Eloise said. "See you tomorrow night."

She waved and walked off. Mademoiselle Dubois hit the key code to enter her apartment. She was so flustered from what had happened earlier, and so glad to be back home, she didn't notice the man passing slowly behind her, eyes focused on the keypad.

Mademoiselle Dubois trudged up the stairs to her third-floor apartment, suddenly exhausted. Yes, a hot bath, and her sister had already promised to bring some wine. They'd order something. She didn't have the strength to cook tonight.

Lost in her own thoughts, she barely said hello to the old woman on the second floor who was just coming out of her apartment to go shopping, and she didn't notice the soft *beep beep beep beep* of the keypad downstairs being punched with the right code.

And the sound of someone coming up the stairs behind her barely registered too. This was a busy building, with people of all ages and several who worked the night shift like her, so there were always people walking around until late at night.

And that made her feel safe. No one would get attacked in this building. There were too many witnesses.

That didn't stop that American madman, she thought with a little shiver. *He was going to kill me right in the middle of a busy cabaret.*

Yes, but that American madman is behind bars. You're safe. You just have the jitters, like Eloise said.

She came to her door, and automatically looked over her shoulder to check if anyone was there like she did any time she entered her apartment. A few years ago, one of her friends had been assaulted by a man who had waited until she had unlocked her door, and then pushed her inside the apartment. Ever since, Mademoiselle Dubois had made this simple precaution.

The only person she saw was a man she didn't recognize going up the stairs at the far end of the hall, carrying a bottle of wine and a bouquet of flowers.

Someone upstairs must be going on a date.

She let herself in, flicked on the lights, and locked the door behind her.

Then she leaned against the door for a moment and collected herself.

Maybe her parents had been right all those years ago. Maybe a move to a big city wasn't for her.

She had been born Bleuenn Heusaff in a little town in Brittany, an out of the way fishing port swept by the waves and the wind. A town where most girls did nothing more than marry a local fisherman or shopkeeper. A woman who wanted a career could open a shop, be a schoolteacher, or go into the regional government and work in an office tallying fishing statistics.

Her mother had married a fisherman, and while her father was a good man who provided for his family and loved his wife, it was obvious that her mother had wanted more from her lie. Bleuenn could see it in her eyes every time she read a fashion magazine or watched a show on television about Paris or Rome or London, any of the big cities where something was happening.

Because nothing ever happened in their little town. Ever.

Still, her mother had been cautious when Bleuenn announced the day she graduated high school that she would move to Paris to become an entertainer. Bleuenn had starred in all the school plays and even had a small part in a TV movie filmed not far from their town on Brittany's rugged coast.

"The big city can be dangerous," her mother had said. "And you don't know anyone."

“Paris is a place of bad morals,” her father had said, sitting in his armchair and smoking his pipe. “You need to be careful. Stay here where decent people live.”

Nevertheless, her parents had not objected too long or too strongly. A buoyant, happy girl with an obvious talent for acting, singing, and dancing, they knew that a little Breton fishing port was no place for her. If she stayed, she’d wither. So they wiped their tears, gave her as much money as they could afford, and bought her a one-way ticket to Paris.

The one-way ticket had been her mother’s idea.

“Don’t weaken,” she had whispered to her on their last breakfast together. “If you decide to chase your dream, don’t stop part of the way.”

Bleuenn had given her mother a kiss, tears forming in her eyes at the thought of her mother, once a young woman like herself, setting aside her own dreams.

So Bleuenn would go to Paris, and she would make herself a success. Not just for herself, but for that young woman her mother had once been.

It hadn’t been easy. Paris was filled with talented, beautiful women trying to find jobs in entertainment. Bleuenn called up the talent agency that had originally gotten her the role in the TV movie. Through them she got on a commercial, plus a couple of jobs as an extra in TV movies. And then nothing. She supported herself as a waitress and kept searching. The words of her mother stuck in her head, and for two years she didn’t have a single bite, until she heard of an audition for a cabaret at the Montparnasse Follies.

Remembering her father’s words, she asked around among her singer and dancer friends and learned that it wasn’t a bad place. No drugs, and no prostitution. Of course, if the entertainers wanted to meet the guests and go home with them after the show, that was their business, but it wasn’t required.

She had gone to the audition and her heart had sunk to her feet. There must have been two hundred other women there. How could she get the role?

To her amazement, she did. Monsieur Duplantier had said she was brilliant! Stunning! Beautiful! The greatest fresh talent he had ever seen in thirty years in showbusiness!

Then he had offered her a starting salary only marginally higher than what she made waiting tables.

Still, it was a job, and it was regular. And many men sent gifts. Flowers, silk scarves, jewelry, even cash. She never gave them anything in return other than sincere thanks and a conversation over a bottle of champagne, but the gifts kept coming. She even had two or three regulars, older men who came at least once a week and would talk with her, always giving her a little something as a token of their appreciation.

Bleuenn Heusaff, now Mademoiselle Dubois, slowly began to realize that while these lonely older men would have loved to enjoy her body, a simple smile and an hour of pleasant conversation was enough for them. Oh, there were a few stray hands, but a light slap on the wrist and they withdrew. If they didn't, she did. She was no whore, despite the risqué act she put on.

She undressed while her bath filled, the rush of the water the only sound she could hear. As she let herself into the steaming water and let out a moan of relaxed pleasure, the last trickle of water covered up the soft *click click click* of a lockpick being jiggled in her front door.

And she did not hear the soft tread of a man tiptoeing through her living room, nor did she see him peek through the open bathroom door.

Her eyes remained closed as she luxuriated in the bath …

… then snapped open as she heard a footstep in her bathroom.

A burly man stood at the foot of her bath. He looked German, with short blonde hair and blue eyes. Laughing eyes. Laughing at her.

In his hand he gripped a thin steel spike sharpened to a fine point.

Bleuenn screamed. The man rushed at her, grasped her blonde hair, and shoved her head below the surface of the water. With his other hand he drove the spike into her body.

She screamed again, and sucked in water.

As she writhed and struggled, she choked on the lungful of bathwater and jerked every time that cold steel spike drove into her abdomen.

A marlinspike, she realized. *Like the sailors use. Like father uses.*

That was her last thought before darkness enveloped her.

Bleuenn Heusaff, famous among Parisian aficionados of the cabaret as Mademoiselle Dubois, died never understanding why this man wanted to hurt her.

CHAPTER TWENTY ONE

Alexa and Stuart lounged in the processing area of one of the main Parisian police stations while the gendarmes took Brent Richter's fingerprints and photographs. Astrid busied herself elsewhere with a mountain of forms. The gendarmes, despite their earlier skepticism, took their being proven wrong with grace. They had even brought in a bottle of wine for Alexa and Stuart to share. Policework was a bit different in France.

Not that she was complaining. The wine was exquisite, and even though she was still technically on duty, she felt she had earned it. She raised her glass and clinked it across the table with her partner.

"Here's to another case solved," she said.

"We make a good team," he replied with a smile.

Their gaze lingered on each other for a moment. Alexa felt a warmth inside her she hadn't felt in a long time. It was so nice having a partner who she could trust and rely on. And he was a good guy too. Kind and caring. Annette was really missing out on someone special, the silly party girl.

Her phone buzzed.

"I'm going to ignore that," she declared. "Pour me another glass, please."

"I will," Stuart said, picking up the bottle, "but I think you should answer that."

"Work can wait until tomorrow. I'm going to finish this bottle with you, go to the hotel, and sleep for twelve hours."

"That's not a work call," Stuart told her, smiling.

She picked up her phone and saw Stacy had sent her a text. Her heart lifted.

"I told her the case was finished," Stuart said, "and how much you kicked ass. Then I told her I'd be mad if she didn't text you."

"Oh my God, thank you!"

The message read, "Good job! When are you coming home?"

Alexa texted back. "Probably in a day or two. I guess there will be some paperwork."

Stacy: "Why do cops have to do paperwork?"

Alexa: "Everyone has to do paperwork. It's one of the curses of adulthood."

Stacy: "Like stretch marks? ☺"

Alexa: "Watch it."

Stacy: "Smith and Wesson are doing good."

Alexa: "You do a great job taking care of them."

Stacy. "Thx. CPS came back."

Alexa: "What did they say?"

Stacy: "Nothing. Just asked a bunch of the same questions."

Alexa: "Were your parents mad?"

Stacy: "A bit. Not at me, though. So when are you coming home?"

Alexa: "In a day or two. I told you."

Stacy: "I told my friends you were doing an international case. You're like a total heroin."

Alexa: "Heroine."

Stacy: "???"

Alexa: "A heroine is a female hero. Heroin is the drug."

Stacy: "I'll remember that when I order some from the school dealer. JOKE!!!"

Astrid walked up to them with a bundle of forms

. "We need to fill these out. Then we can go to hotel. I need some sleep."

"Same here," Stuart said.

Alexa took a photo of the pile of paperwork and sent it to Stacy with the note, "I have to fill out all this stuff before hitting the sack. Talk to you tomorrow."

Stacy: "OK. Make sure it doesn't give you stretch marks. :-D."

Alexa: "Wiseass."

She put away her phone, leaned over the desk, and gave Stuart a hug.

"Oh! What's this for?" he asked, hugging her back.

"For being wonderful. Thanks so much."

Stuart held her tighter. Gently Alexa released him, troubled by the sensation being close to him had brought out. She sat back down, coughed, and said,

"Let's get to work on this stuff, eh?"

They busied themselves with the forms, which were in French. Luckily the local police sent over someone to help them translate. It was a slow and annoying project, as all police paperwork was, and it didn't help that she was mildly drunk and half asleep.

But none of that bothered her one bit. Stacy had calmed down, and now things could return to normal.

No, not normal. Normal hadn't helped the kid. After the runaway attempt, the school and the CPS were on alert. Now was the chance to face her problems squarely and start fixing them.

She'd be back home soon, and she could get to work.

* * *

Alexa's phone ripped her out of her sleep in the dead of night. She groaned and turned over, tempted to ignore it. The case was done. It was probably some bureaucrat complaining some form hadn't been filled out properly. Well, he could wait until the damn morning.

The phone kept ringing. With a curse, Alexa groped through the darkness to find it. It was Astrid calling. The time was two in the morning. Alexa had gotten a grand total of an hour and a half of sleep.

"What is it?" Alexa demanded, none too politely.

"Mademoiselle Dubois has been murdered."

Alexa sat bolt upright in bed. "What?"

"Someone picked the lock on her apartment door and stabbed her to death in the back. Numerous stab wounds with a short piercing object to the abdomen."

"That's impossible! Richter is in jail!"

"I don't understand it either. We need to get to the crime scene."

* * *

Alexa couldn't believe her bloodshot eyes. The body lay on a stretcher on the bathroom floor, the local homicide squad having already taken crime scene photos. Her bare midriff was a punctured ruin of stab wounds. The bath water was a deep crimson, and there were bloodstains all over the tiled walls and floor.

Two large footprints, about size ten or eleven, were clearly stamped in the pools of blood.

He would have noticed those, and he didn't bother to wipe them away. Why not? Does he want to take risks too?

We couldn't have a copycat already, could we? The murders barely got in the news over the in States, and I don't think the European media has reported it at all. Astrid didn't mention anything.

But it is a copycat. The M.O. is exactly the same. Even down to the same victim.

"Did Mademoiselle Dubois have any enemies?" she asked the room. "Does the cabaret have any links to organized crime?"

One of the gendarmes knew English and answered. "Not that we know of. And the Montparnasse Follies has a good reputation. It isn't a front for prostitution and doesn't have any links with organized crime. It is one of the few such places that keeps itself clean."

"So how did this happen?" Alexa asked, utterly baffled.

"Your serial killer must have a partner in crime."

"But who? We tracked down both siblings and neither is anywhere near Europe."

"Then it must be someone else," the gendarme said. "Perhaps he has a friend here, someone he kills with. It is not unknown for serial killers to have partners."

Alexa nodded. Police records had plenty of examples of that. She'd even come up against one of her own. Drake Logan had a whole following, becoming a sort of cult leader among twisted individuals who aspired to kill for no reason other than their own egos.

So Brent Richter had a partner? They hadn't had any indication of that so far, but then again they'd only realized they were dealing with a serial killer a few days ago.

Alexa yawned and rubbed her eyes. A few days ago? It felt like a few years. The team back in Arizona hadn't even had time to do much beyond get in touch with the family. Richter's father had been dead for years, his mother vanished, and his brother and sister lived off a large inheritance. Neither had spoken to their sibling since the death of their father. They also had no idea of the whereabouts of their mother. After their father had died, she had cut off all ties and had gone away.

The team back in Arizona was trying to trace her. So far no luck. Like her serial killer son, she had used her wealth to vanish. Most likely she had gone to some Third World nation where she could lay low and not be bothered.

But why? Why did she need to run?

The only other thing they'd received was a report from Annette with some fingerprints and hair samples that matched those found in

Brent's home. No other fingerprints or hair samples had been found on the murder scene that could be tied to the murders. Being such public places, of course there were plenty more, but Annette had checked these and hadn't found any individuals that had been at more than one murder scene.

So he had done the U.S. murders alone. Had he fled to Europe not just to escape justice, but to link up with this other killer?

If so, he hadn't used his email account or phone. Those records didn't show any such contact. Thus they had no idea who this new killer might be.

"Back to square one," she muttered.

"Not quite," Stuart said from the doorway. "Brent must know this guy. Let's go wake him up and make him sing."

CHAPTER TWENTY TWO

Stuart studied the killer's face as he sat on the bunk of his jail cell in an isolated section of the city police station. Being so late at night, he still hadn't been transferred to a proper prison. Brent Richter looked worn out, obviously having enjoyed even less sleep than Stuart or Alexa, but even so he seemed perky, with a smug expression on his face that said, "I know more than you do."

Stuart would like to slap that smug expression right off of that face.

He glanced at Alexa, unsure how to proceed. She looked at a loss too. The latest murder had completely blindsided them both.

Astrid wasn't with them. She was conferring with the French police, who had suddenly become a lot more cooperative after the murder of Mademoiselle Dubois.

Brent Richter stared at them, that smug smile growing.

"So who is he?" Stuart asked.

"Who is who?" Brent asked in wide-eyed innocence.

"Don't get cute with us. Someone just murdered Mademoiselle Dubois the same way you murdered the other women."

"Mmmm … " Richter leaned back against the wall, eyes closed and making a noise like he had just tasted something delicious.

He didn't look surprised at all. On the contrary, he looked smug as hell.

Think fast. What would trigger this guy?

"He messed it up, though," Stuart hurried to add. "Mademoiselle Dubois wasn't a blonde. She wore a wig. She actually has short black hair. And she was in the tub, not wearing her red dress at all. So that's strike one and two, isn't it?"

Richter opened his eyes and glared at him.

"An amateur," Stuart declared. "The initial report from the coroner said she didn't even die from the stab wounds. She drowned first. I guess that's strike three, eh? Hardly a worthy successor to a killing machine like you. You need to pick your sidekicks better."

While Stuart hated being so flippant about that poor woman, he needed to get this guy riled up, make him admit who and where the second killer was.

Instead, Richter said only, "You're lying."

"Lying? No, I'm not. I'd show you the crime scene photos but you'd probably start touching yourself. I got to say that girl you found is an amateur."

A brief tug of a smile on Richter's face told him the killer was a man. They'd already thought that based on the shoe size. It was good to confirm, though, and Brent's reaction just confirmed it.

"So who's the next target?" Alexa demanded. "Or is your sidekick just going to wander around Paris looking for another blonde in a red dress?"

Again the fishing worked. No reaction this time except one of determination. So the sidekick wasn't planning on leaving Paris. Interesting.

But why Paris? Convenience, or something more?

"You been following Mademoiselle Dubois a long time? Big fan?" Stuart asked.

Brent made a dismissive wave of his hand. "Never heard of the bitch before I came here. She's not important."

"Important enough to lose your freedom over," Alexa said.

Richter snorted. "I've never been free. I am now."

Odd thing to say.

"Free?" Stuart said. "You're going to prison for the rest of your life. You'll probably serve a sentence here first before going back for your sentence in the States. But I don't think you'll make it back to the good old U S of A. German-American who kills a Frenchwoman? Your cellmates aren't going to like that. They'll probably shiv you or strangle you with a blanket. It happens a lot. Or maybe they'll just pass you around like a pack of smokes. Or maybe that's why you want to go to jail? Be the lady of the cellblock? I'll send you a blonde wig and a red dress to wear."

Richter's glare heated up. "You're not going to bait me into saying anything, pig."

Stuart shrugged. "Because you have nothing to say. You think you're some criminal mastermind? All you did was stab a few helpless women, and the only reason you got away with it for so long was mommy and daddy's money."

A spark of rage. Richter bared his teeth.

Interesting.

Stuart felt a touch on his hand. Alexa.

He turned to her and she nodded toward the cellblock door.

Together they walked out. Once the guard shut the door behind them and Richter couldn't hear, Stuart asked, "So what do you think?"

"He can maintain a lot of self-control, but that mention of his parents really got to him."

"Yeah, I noticed that too," Stuart said. "Maybe we can work with that. Maybe it's the mother he's lashing out at. He wouldn't be the first serial killer with mother issues."

Alexa nodded. They had both dealt with enough of these cases to know that most serial killers suffered years of childhood abuse, twisting their psychologies and warping their sense of wrong and right.

"If only we knew where the mother went," Stuart said. "The latest news from stateside is they still can't track her down. She seems to have changed her name and used her money to hide her tracks. I'm thinking she's scared of this guy. Maybe he attacked her before, when he was younger, and she realized she had created a monster."

The partners lapsed into silence. After a minute, Alexa snapped her fingers.

"I have an idea," Alexa said. She headed out to the main office, Stuart following.

They found Astrid talking with one of the French homicide detectives, a thin man with a handlebar moustache, while they drink very tempting cups of espresso.

"Would you like some coffee?" the German officer asked as they came up.

"I'd love some," Alexa said, "but first I'm wondering if you'd mind reprising your role as a blonde woman in a red dress."

"To be bait again?" This idea didn't seem to phase her at all.

"Not quite. I want you to present yourself to Richter and see if that sets him off. He's not responding to questioning and this might get him to snap."

"An excellent idea," the homicide detective said, wiping his moustache free of some drops of coffee.

"Now we just need a red dress," Alexa said, looking around the Spartan interior of the police station.

The homicide detective coughed, rubbed one side of his moustache and then the other, and said, "Well, we do have Mademoiselle Dubois's dress in the evidence room."

The murdered woman's dress? Stuart doubted Astrid would want to put that on.

There was a pause. Finally the German officer said, "I'll do it."

The homicide detective took her to the evidence room, then she went to the bathroom with the dress. A minute later she emerged, looking as uncomfortable as if she wore a dress woven out of worms.

Together they went back to Richter's cell.

"Maybe pretend to be his mother," Stuart suggested. "When I mentioned his parents he got really pissed."

"I'll try that."

As they entered the cell block, Stuart and Alexa hung back enough to let Astrid do her work, but close enough to see Richter's reaction.

That reaction was dramatic and immediate.

As soon as Astrid walked within view with her blonde hair and red dress, Richter leapt up and gripped the bars of his cell, pushing his face against the bars as if he could squeeze through.

"What's this? What are you doing?" Brent demanded.

"Brent," Astrid cooed, "It's been so long. How are you, my boy?"

"What? Why are you talking like that, cop?"

"I know things went wrong with us," she continued in a sweet voice. "I'm sorry I wasn't a better mother, but I love you and forgive you."

"Get the hell out of here!" Brent shouted, rattling the door of his cell.

"But son, we can start again. Be mother and—"

"We'll kill you! You can't hide from us. Konrad and I—"

Brent cut himself off, his face showing shock that soon transformed back to hatred.

Even when you screw up yourself, you blame other people, don't you? So typical of a criminal.

Brent slowly backed away from the cell door. The back of his legs hit the bunk and he sat down hard. For a moment his eyes moved away, looking everywhere except at Astrid and the two American officers. Then they seemed to gain confidence and looked right back at the apparition in the red dress.

"You'll never catch him in time. You're going to die, mother. We were going to kill you together, bathe in your blood, but if he gets you alone, that's good enough. We'll be free of you. We'll never have to hear you again."

He hears her in his head, Stuart realized.

Brent lapsed into silence, crossing his arms and putting on a smug expression.

"Let's go," Alexa said. She and Astrid walked down the hall. Stuart lingered behind.

"Who's Konrad? A friend? Extended family?"

Silence.

"What did she do to you?"

Silence.

"Whatever she did, it sounds pretty bad. She was wrong to hurt you. But this isn't the way to put the past behind you."

A short, derisive laugh. Brent looked away.

Stuart, knowing he'd get no more from the prisoner, went to catch up with the other two officers.

When he got to the main office of the police station, Astrid had already disappeared, in a hurry to get out of the dead woman's dress. Alexa was already on the phone.

"We got to pull put all the stops to track the mother down," she said as the phone rang. "It helps that we know she's probably in the Paris area. We'll try to track down this Konrad too."

"I'm thinking he's extended family," Stuart said. "A childhood friend wouldn't have stuck around for the abuse. Let's check if anyone else was under the mother's care. You track down the mother and I'll talk to Brent's siblings, see if anyone else lived in the house."

"Right." She started talking to whoever had answered the phone.

Stuart hurried to another phone. He needed to make a round of calls to Brent's family. They hadn't been exactly forthcoming before. Now he needed answers, and he needed them fast.

CHAPTER TWENTY THREE

This was the place. After all the searching, all those years, he had finally found it.

He'd found her hiding place three times before, but the bitch moved around so much he'd always made it there too late.

Now he was sure. She was in there. She hadn't left.

Konrad Richter took a deep breath and scanned the building in the bucolic countryside not far outside Paris. It was one of those stately homes built in the eighteenth century, an impressive stone building with tall windows, three stories, and an east wing and west wing each larger than most modern apartment buildings. It was reached through an expansive front garden complete with a hedge maze, a couple of dozen flowerbeds, and an enormous fountain of putti riding dolphins that shot out streams of water from their mouths.

The Countess Frieda Richter did not live here by herself. Even she wasn't rich enough to afford the whole place. Like most of the old stately homes of Europe, it had long ceased serving as a private residence. Now it was a retirement home for the wealthy. From what he could learn from the Internet, some forty elderly millionaires lived here, cared for by a small army of nurses, cooks, butlers and drivers.

Not a bad place to end your days. And the Countess Frieda Richter's days were just about over.

Getting to the building would be a problem, though. The long driveway up to the palace was blocked by an ornate ironwork fence, and the entire property was encircled by a high brick wall. A team of well-trained security guards patrolled the property day and night. The elderly residents had a lot of Rolexes and pricey jewelry. A place like this was a burglar's wet dream.

So it was well set up to guard against burglars. He would have to find another way.

Konrad Richter forced himself to move on. It was the early hours of the morning and the gate had not yet opened. Dressed in khaki shorts, hiking boots, and with a backpack on his back, he was playing the part of a hiker. Conveniently, a national trail passed right by the property, leading through the Marne River valley and passing several World War One battlefields.

How appropriate. Living with that woman had left him shell shocked.

His own parents, the countess's playboy brother and his coke-snorting wife who was technically Konrad's mother although she had never acted like it, had lived a jet setting lifestyle that didn't include their only child. Instead they had foisted him off to his Uncle Otto and Aunt Frieda. His mother and father had been only too glad to get rid of him so they could go off and party in the Maldives.

Konrad was convinced he had been an accident. Ironic that the only thing they had ever done right they had done accidentally.

If he had felt ignored and unwanted in his parents' house, staying with Aunt Frieda was ten times worse. There he wasn't ignored. Oh no, far from it.

Him and his older cousin Brent were the subject of far too much attention.

Uncle Otto wasn't the problem. He was just a distant uncaring drunk like his own father. It was Aunt Frieda that was the real evil of his childhood.

Konrad walked on the path running along the River Marne, oblivious to the quiet morning, the cheery birdsong, and the rising sun dappling the river with gold. Instead of enjoying the nature like all the other hikers who came along this national trail, he got flung back into his childhood, consumed by the old tension and old hatred.

Although Aunt Frieda had rarely hit him, and had never touched him inappropriately, she had wrecked his childhood and left in him a lifelong rage that could only be soothed by avenging himself on the person who had made his younger years a misery.

That revenge would come soon. First he needed to pitch his tent at a government campground just a couple of kilometers down the trail. That would be his excuse to linger. There were several sites of historical and natural interest to see in the area, and hikers often stayed for several days. No one would take the least notice of him as he scouted the retirement home and its grounds. By the time Brent made it here, he'd be prepared.

Because Brent deserved to be in on this. His cousin had suffered even more than Konrad. The poor bastard had to live with Aunt Frieda full time. Considering how deep her claws had gotten into Konrad's head from just four or five months a year for a few years, it was a miracle that Brent was as functional as he was.

"Humiliation," Konrad growled out loud. "Pure, deliberate humiliation."

A movement out of the corner of his eye made him look. An elderly fisherman sat on the nearby riverbank, staring at him. When he saw Konrad looking he quickly looked back at his fishing rod and made a show of adjusting it.

I have to be careful with that, Konrad told himself. *I vocalize too damn much.*

At least he had spoken in German. Hopefully that French senior citizen couldn't understand.

Konrad continued on his way, fuming as laughter rang in his ears.

Not laughter from the old man, laughter from Aunt Frieda.

She was always laughing at him. Sneering at every failure. Pointing out every shortcoming. Laughing in that nasty, cutting way of hers every time he came up short.

Not real laughter. He hadn't seen Aunt Frieda since he was sixteen. It was laughter in his head. Ghost laughter. Demon laughter. He was possessed by demon laughter.

So was Brent, and when he got here they'd become exorcists.

Look at you two, Aunt Frieda screeched. *Tweedle Dumb and Tweedle Dumber. Do these dishes look clean to you? No wonder my brother doesn't want you around, Konrad. You're just as useless as Brent. And don't whine that you're too young. You're ten. I was washing plenty of dishes when I was ten.*

Konrad shook himself, blinked, and looked around him. Sometimes he got lost in scenes from the past. He saw the turnoff for the campsite and took it. As he arrived at a clearing in the woods not far from the river, he saw only a couple of other campers, one already striking his tent in preparation for moving on. Good.

His body shifted to automatic, going through the motions of pitching his tent as his thoughts once again cast back to the bitter past.

Washing dishes. Like she had ever washed a dish in her life. And he shouldn't have had to either. They had a cleaning lady for that. She came in every day, but never had much work to do thanks to that slave driver of an aunt. He and Brent would scrub floors, wash windows, and clean the toilet.

The toilet was her favorite chore to assign, usually after vomiting into it to clear her body of the previous night's binge drinking. She'd wait a while, leaving the door and window closed so the bathroom filled with the nasty funk as the vomit congealed into a crusty mass. Then she'd send them in there with nothing more than rags to wipe the gunk off.

It builds character, she'd say with a smarmy smile.

The first time he'd been over at that house, spending a month there when he was nine and Brent was eleven, he'd been so shocked by this psychological onslaught that he had immediately told his parents when he had returned home. His father, usually so distant, had actually showed a trace of concern, and had called his sister to ask what happened.

He's lying, Aunt Frieda said. *I think he stole my emerald earrings. You know the ones I got for my birthday last year? They went missing the day he left.*

His father searched Konrad's overnight bag and sure enough found them hidden in a side pocket. The harpy must have put them in there to entrap him.

You need to get that kid's head examined. I caught him putting them up to his ears like he wanted to wear them. He used my perfume several times too. I think he's a fruit.

That earned Konrad a hard spanking and a lecture about being a "real man."

After that incident, Konrad knew he was helpless.

Helpless, but not on his own, and not broken.

He had Brent, and he had the time when he wasn't in Aunt Frieda's house to give him strength. Even at that tender age he could see that Brent's having to deal with that relentless onslaught of spite had broken his spirit. Konrad made it his mission to revive it.

It started small. Watering down Aunt Frieda's gin, or adding a bit of pee to the whiskey. Breaking a favorite piece of china when she was passed out so she would think she'd done it herself. He became a child prodigy in subtle means of harassment.

His older cousin watched all this with a mixture of admiration and horror. When Konrad had put a bit of one of his turds in Aunt Frieda's chocolate mousse, the poor kid even peed himself.

He had to admit that had gone too far. He'd almost gotten caught with that stunt. When Aunt Frieda had taken it out of the fridge (meaning only to eat it herself, in front of them, yet another of her little tortures), she had sniffed it and grumbled that it had gone off. For a moment he and Brent had frozen in terror, convinced she'd put two and two together, but her booze-addled mind hadn't made the connection.

After that he grew more careful, and more dissatisfied. He wanted to hurt her, like she hurt them, but couldn't think of anything that he could do that would be big enough to even the score but subtle enough to get away with.

Until the day he snapped.

He was fourteen then. Brent was sixteen. Brent's older siblings had moved out, both taking off the instant they turned eighteen. Konrad had been stuck at his uncle and aunt's house for three weeks while his parents went off somewhere. He didn't know where. They had stopped bothering to tell him.

The rage had been building in them both. They had confided in each other that they sometimes heard her voice in their heads even when she wasn't around. They found themselves reacting to her as if she was right there. If they dropped something, or bombed a math test, it would be like she was just over their shoulder, criticizing them.

Brent seemed to have that worse. Konrad sometimes caught him whispering to his mother when she wasn't around, defending himself, or saying all the things he didn't dare say to her face.

And one day, no worse but certainly no better than any other, Konrad decided he had had enough.

He was a minor, he realized, and that meant while there would be consequences for doing what he really wanted to do, he wouldn't serve any time. Probably go to a juvenile psych ward or something.

That could be no worse than his aunt's house.

So he bided his time all day, cleaning toilets, enduring taunts, until as usual Aunt Frieda drank herself into a stupor with a bottle of urine-infused whiskey.

And then he had gone down to the kitchen, Brent tagging along, and got the biggest, sharpest knife he could find.

"What are you going to do with that?" Brent asked, fear making his voice waver.

"What do you think?" he asked, stomping out of the kitchen and trying not to let his hands shake.

“Are you going to cut up all those new dresses she bought today?” Brent asked and snickered. Even though he was older, he had been acting more and more like his bolder cousin’s sidekick.

“No.”

“Are you going to cut off all her hair?”

“No.”

They were going up the stairs now, Konrad growing determined, Brent tagging behind.

“Then … what are you going to do?”

Brent’s question came out as barely a whisper.

“You know,” Konrad replied.

“My dad might be home soon,” Brent said. The words came out in a rush, as if he wanted to make excuses.

“So?”

“He’ll find out. Somebody will find out!”

“Yeah. So? They can’t put me in jail. I’m still a kid.”

“But—”

Konrad rounded on his cousin, making him stop so quickly he almost stumbled down the steps.

“Look, if you’re too much of a wuss, don’t come with me.”

Brent flushed and looked at his feet. “I am a wuss, aren’t I?”

Immediately Konrad felt sorry. That what his aunt always called Brent. She called Konrad that too.

“You’re not a wuss. But I don’t think you can handle this. That’s OK. I’ll do it. I’ll say you tried to stop me.”

The cousins looked at each other for a moment. When Brent didn’t say anything, Konrad went up the last of the steps and walked down the hall to Aunt Frieda’s bedroom.

The door was closed. Konrad paused a moment, listening. Then he knocked softly. Brent sucked in his breath.

No answer. Summoning his courage, Konrad opened the door.

Aunt Frieda lay sprawled at an angle on the king-sized our-poster bed. A whiskey bottle, nearly empty, sat on the bedside table along with some of her pills.

Good. Konrad wasn’t sure what those pills were, but he knew they made her sleep more deeply.

Even so, he found himself walking on tiptoe as he moved over to the bed. Aunt Frieda lay with her head toward him, chin slightly back, exposing the throat.

Konrad paused, heart thundering in his chest. How to do this? Did he slice her throat? How much strength did that take? The movies made it look easy, but those were only movies. Maybe he should stab her. That might be easier. He'd have more leverage.

Konrad turned the knife around so it pointed down. He held it with both hands, then realized his palms were sweaty and he wiped them on his jeans.

"We're going to get caught," Brent whispered from the doorway. He hadn't dared enter the room.

"You want to be treated like crap the rest of your life?"

Brent didn't reply. Konrad raised the knife higher. Even with her asleep he felt scared of her.

Not for much longer.

He brought the knife down.

CHAPTER TWENTY FOUR

If only it had ended there, Konrad thought as he finished setting up his tent.

Just at the moment he brought the knife down to pierce that shrieking throat, Aunt Frieda shifted on the bed and opened her eyes.

Konrad squawked and his hands jerked. The knife embedded in the mattress.

His aunt leapt out of bed, eyes wide with terror. For a moment everyone stood in their places, no one saying anything, before the two boys fled the room.

They hid behind the boiler in the cellar, too terrified to move.

Uncle Otto came home within an hour, obviously having been called by Aunt Frieda, who had no doubt locked herself in some upstairs room. From their hiding place in the basement they heard his Cadillac pull up, Uncle Otto run into the house, and the two of them leaving. Uncle Otto and Aunt Frieda drove off, leaving the two boys alone in the mansion.

No one came for three days. Uncle Otto had apparently told the staff not to come. Konrad and Brent didn't bother going to school. The school never called. Konrad guessed the adults had told the school they were both sick. So they watched TV, played video games, and emptied the fridge. When all the food was gone, they had to scrounge around Uncle Otto's drawers to find some cash to order a pizza.

Even so, by the third day they were getting hungry. That's when Konrad's parents arrived. A slap, a curt order to get packed, and he was taken away to a group home.

He never saw his older cousin or his aunt or uncle again. He spent two years in a group home getting lectured by a psychologist who didn't believe a word of his side of the story. "Konrad, even if someone is a little harsh, trying to do them physical harm is inappropriate."

The betrayal cut deep. No one believed him. Not his parents, not the staff at the group home. No one. It plunged him into a well of loneliness and mistrust that he could never climb out of.

Even worse, he was considered the bad one. Her voice echoed through his head, cackling with victory.

It wasn't until years later that he tracked Brent down. He made contact, and found that Brent still savored a deep hatred for his mother, just as Konrad did. Konrad still wanted to finish what he had started that day so long ago, and now he had the courage. He had practiced on neighborhood pets before moving up to homeless people and eventually prostitutes. He now knew how to draw a knife across a throat, and he knew how to keep his hands steady.

Konrad Richter was ready.

The only problem was, Aunt Frieda had changed her name and disappeared. None of her family had heard from her in years.

Had she realized that someday her son and nephew, all grown up, would come after her?

It took years to find her. Konrad hired private detectives, the kind that will keep quiet for some extra cash, and even so it was a long search. Aunt Frieda had covered her tracks well.

But eventually one of the detectives had found her, living as Inge Pedersen and pretending to be Danish, in this ritzy old age home not far outside Paris.

Konrad had contacted Brent and told him the news.

That had been a mistake. When he heard, Brent flipped out and went on a killing spree.

Not that there was anything wrong with that, but he kept going after women who looked like his mother, and he boasted about how many risks he took just to prove he could get away with it.

Idiot. Still trying to get approval from his mother, by killing women who looked like her and eluding the police.

Why couldn't he kill people nobody cared about? That way you could kill and kill and no one would be any the wiser. Konrad had made a study of serial killers. The ones who racked up the highest body count were those who killed the homeless and prostitutes. Stabbing women at swank parties in country clubs was a good way to get yourself caught.

Get Konrad caught too.

Still, he couldn't deny Brent the chance to be in on this final murder. He was his cousin, after all, the only real family he ever had. They'd do it together, like they should have all those years ago. Brent was due here today. It would be good to see him again. And once they'd done what they needed to do, they could disappear to some Third World country and live off the money they had in various secret bank accounts.

The sound of the news coming over the radio caught his attention. The camper at the other end of the clearing had a small portable radio tuned to the morning news program.

"Brent Richter, a German-American suspected of several slayings in the United States, was apprehended by police last night in Paris as he attempted to attack a dancer at the Montparnasse Follies in downtown …"

Try as he might, Konrad couldn't focus on the rest. He staggered into his tent and curled up out of sight. His cousin had gotten himself caught. The idiot! Brent was always soft, always sloppy, ruined by that bitch.

Now it was up to him.

And he had to hurry. He didn't think his cousin would rat him out, but they'd be on the trail after Konrad had killed that cabaret dancer.

That had been a mistake. Brent had told him about the dancer and how he was going to go for her. The original plan was to follow her home. Konrad had decided to follow her home too, thinking that they could have a joyous reunion as they stabbed her together. When Konrad hadn't seen Brent around, he had figured he'd gotten delayed or scared off or something. He didn't think Brent would be dumb enough to try and kill her in the actual theater in front of all those people.

Brent had wanted to get caught. Poor guy. Still wanting to get punished. Still the target for disapproval.

Not Konrad. He was going to end the cycle. He was going to come out on top. He'd do it for his own sanity, and for his poor, useless cousin.

She broke you, buddy, but I'm going to break her.

Konrad zipped up the tent and unpacked his backpack. Inside he had a Fedex uniform and a package he had carefully printed with the address of the retirement home and the name Inge Pedersen, with the return address of his cousin Hans in Thailand. He had a second uniform for Brent, now unnecessary. He'd murdered that second Fedex agent for nothing. Ah, well. You got to break a few eggs to make an omelet, as the Americans say.

He put on the uniform, struggling in the cramped confines of the tent. Then he picked up the package. He didn't worry about the fact that his aunt would be alerted by Hans supposedly knowing her alias. He only needed it to get through the front door. By the time she saw the package it would be too late.

He checked the slim box. It was open, but he could hold the seam closed with his hand and no one would notice. Inside was a garrote made of two wooden pegs at each end of a length of piano wire. Unlike his more bloodthirsty cousin, he preferred to strangle his victims. It was fun to feel them thrash around like a fish out of water. He'd only stabbed that dancer out of courtesy to Brent.

Once dressed, he unzipped the tent and peeked out. The guy with the radio was still there, sitting in a camp chair and reading a novel. He was a stocky, middle-aged man with graying hair that had already retreated from much of his scalp. Probably one of those casual hikers who only do ten or twelve kilometers a day. It didn't look like he planned on leaving anytime soon.

Damn. This was a problem. Konrad scanned the rest of the campground. The other camper had left and this early in the morning no one else had shown up.

The reader glanced up and saw Konrad, who nodded to him and ducked back into his tent.

I can't walk past him in a Fedex uniform. That will attract attention.

But I don't have time to change back into civilian clothes, pack up the disguise, and change back into it in the bushes or somewhere. I need to get over there now. It might already be too late.

I guess I'll just have to do what I do.

Grabbing the package, Konrad stepped out of the tent.

The reader was back to his novel and didn't look up. As Konrad walked for him, he glanced around the clearing. No one in sight. Good.

He got halfway across the clearing before the hiker looked up from his book. His face registered surprise to see Konrad in a Fedex uniform and carrying a package while heading for his tent.

"Delivery for you," Konrad said in French.

The man laughed. "You like your job so much that you hike in your uniform?"

"No, I hate my job so much that I pack my uniform so I can stay out in the woods longer. I have a shift starting soon."

The man's brow furrowed in confusion. Konrad was almost to him now.

"But you're not French." The note of disapproval in his voice was unmistakable.

"I moved here from Germany a couple of years ago. The EU lets us do that now."

People have been doing that for years. Can't you figure that out, or are you a nationalist? Probably voted for the anti-immigrant party. Well, you'll be no loss to humanity.

Konrad hated racists. He hated anyone who picked on other people.

He stopped beside him. The man hadn't made a move, although he stared at Konrad, confused. Not scared, just confused.

"I got something in here you might like," Konrad said, reaching into the package.

"It's a bit early for a drink," the camper said.

Konrad hooked his fingers around one of the pegs and pulled out the garotte. The man's eyes registered even more confusion, then fear. He dropped his book and began to get up.

Too late. Konrad grabbed the other handle of the garotte and looped the piano wire around the man's neck. The camper made a gurgling sound and grabbed at the wire. All that managed to do was trap a couple of his fingers between the wire and his own neck. Blood oozed from them as Konrad constricted the wire around his victim.

The hiker clawed at the wire with his other hand, instinctively trying to loosen the grip it had on his esophagus.

Then the guy got smart. Subduing his panic, he jammed an elbow into Konrad's stomach. Konrad gritted his teeth and hauled back on the man's neck. Twice more that elbow slammed into his middle, each blow weaker than the one before. The man went back to trying to pull the wire way.

Konrad smiled. When they did that, it was all over. He pressed his knee against the small of the man's back and pulled harder. The guy managed to stomp on Konrad's foot, but there was no stopping him now. Another half a minute, and the man twisted a couple of times and went limp.

Konrad kept the garotte tight for another full minute just to be sure, then dragged him inside his tent. Konrad made a quick scan of the interior and saw no evidence that the Frenchman was with anyone else.

Good. He zipped up the tent, washed the garrote with the man's own canteen and a dried it with the man's towel.

Then Konrad replaced the garotte in the Fedex package and, whistling a happy tune, walked back down the path toward the retirement home. The gate should be open by this hour.

Getting inside would be easy. No one ever suspected a delivery man.

CHAPTER TWENTY FIVE

Alexa had spent a sleepless night trying to track down Frieda Richter. She and Stuart had called every law enforcement agency in the United States, and both surviving siblings.

They had found out only two things—that Frieda Richter had truly vanished and no one knew where she was, and that a cousin named Konrad had spent much of his childhood with Brent after Brent's two older siblings had moved out.

Astrid got to work searching for Konrad, and found that like Brent and Frieda, he too had vanished.

But not as well as the other two. Astrid soon got a lead and found he was living in Cologne. The local police checked his home and discovered him missing. Neighbors said they hadn't seen him in several days. Everyone described him as a personable but quiet man. German police records showed no criminal complaints against him, although he had been questioned in relation to the strangulation death of a homeless man a couple of years before. He had been seen in the area where the man had been killed, but there was no solid evidence to tie him to the murder and he hadn't even been considered a likely suspect.

In the light of current events, Alexa and her team agreed that conclusion needed a serious reassessment.

"I'm thinking he discovered where Frieda was, and that he called Brent to come on over to Europe so they could murder her together," she said.

"They both came to Paris," Stuart replied. "She must be somewhere in or near the city. But where?"

That got answered after several hours of digging. It turned out that Frieda Richter had moved to Denmark for several years, legally changing her name there to Inge Pedersen. After a move to a beachside bungalow in Tunisia for a time, she had moved back to Denmark, then to Italy, and finally to France.

All this they got from customs officials and flight records in the various countries. But once she entered France the trail went cold.

"We can't find any records of her buying or renting property," said a gendarme whose bloodshot eyes showed he had been working as hard as Alexa and her colleagues.

The sun was peeking through the windows now, heralding a new day. Alexa felt sure it wouldn't set without Frieda Richter being murdered, and they had come up on a dead end.

Stuart snapped his fingers. "She's old! She's 73 now! Maybe she's in a retirement home."

"Right!" Alexa said.

Stuart gave her a high five, then clenched her fingers held them for a moment, looking her in the eye.

Whoa! Um ...

"Let's get to work," she said, pulling her hand away.

Alexa, Stuart, Astrid, and the overworked gendarme made a round of calls to all the assisted living facilities in the Greater Paris metro area. This got hampered by the early hour and the lack of French spoken by much of the team. Many places didn't even answer the phone.

As they slowly ticked retirement homes off the list, and tried calling the no answers a second time, they dragged a couple more gendarmes into the phone pool as they arrived for the morning shift.

Alexa grew more and more tense, and every failed call made it worse.

Suddenly, one of the gendarmes leapt up and shouted something in French. Everyone turned to stare at him. He remembered himself and switched to English.

"I found her! A woman named Inge Pedersen moved into the Palais de Montbelliard. I have heard of it. It is an exclusive retirement home in an old palace in the Marne River valley."

They rushed out to their cars, one of the gendarmes calling the local police as he went.

* * *

Getting through the front gate went as smoothly as Konrad thought it would. He walked right up to the two security men, showed a fake Fedex ID he'd made with a laser printer and laminator, and the name on the package, and walked right through.

He continued to whistle the happy tune he'd been whistling since the campsite as he strolled up the magnificent driveway past the fountain. A few elderly residents puttered around the lawn or admired the flowerbeds. A nurse pushed an aged woman on a wheelchair.

As he approached the building, the tune Konrad's whistling faltered and died. His heart began to beat more quickly. The air suddenly felt hot and close. His legs felt like he was dragging them through sludge as he tried to make his way to a front door that suddenly seemed kilometers away.

All those years. It had been half a lifetime since he'd seen her last. His gaze roved across the front lawn, checking every female face, suddenly terrified that he'd meet her out here and not in the privacy of her room.

He stopped by the fountain for a moment, the splashing water cooling the air. He took a deep breath and wiped his brow. As he did so, he let go of the open seam of the package and the end of his garotte fell out. He fumbled the package, stuffed the garotte back in, and fearfully looked around.

No one seemed to have noticed.

Get a hold of yourself. You've waited years for this. Don't mess up like Brent.

"You mess up everything! You're useless! No wonder your parents ditched you with us!"

Squaring his shoulders, Konrad strode to the front steps, climbed them, and passed into the cool marble interior of the entrance hall. A nurse's station stood just inside and to the left. He walked over to it. A woman in a nurse's uniform looked up.

He opened his mouth to speak, only managed a hoarse whisper, cleared his throat, and said, "Package for Mrs. Pedersen."

Konrad felt sure she would get suspicious. He was shaking all over, his voice had been laden with fear, and the old bat had probably never received a package since she'd moved in. She was living in hiding, after all.

But the nurse, who looked bored, didn't seem to notice any of this. She simply made him sign a check-in form and waved toward a grand staircase, the symmetry of its marble banisters ruined by one of those automatic chair lifts running along one of them.

"Room 207. East wing. Go right at the top of the stairs," she said. As if to head off a common question, she added. "The elevator is for staff and residents only."

Konrad nodded and headed for the stairs. He wasn't about to take the elevator anyway, wherever that was. Enclosed spaces left you trapped, and he planned on getting out of here. He'd been cursed with that woman's screeching and constant judging all his life. Any time he did anything, her phantom would loom over his shoulder, clucking its disapproval.

Killing her would kill the phantom too, and he looked forward to finally enjoying a life of peace. He'd stop killing and move to some Third World nation where he could buy anonymity.

Konrad smiled as he ascending the steps. His hands no longer shook and his gait remained steady.

An old man hobbled down the stairs, one hand gripping a cane and the other on the bannister.

"Wonderful day, isn't it?" Konrad said as the man passed.

"Better if you're young," the man croaked.

Young.

Konrad had never been young, not since he had been given a part-time sentence in hell.

Now he had a chance to be young.

His chest puffed out as he got to the top of the stairs. Yes, a new life! No more strangling bums and whores. No more worries about the police. A nice bungalow on a pristine beach somewhere, a cute local maid with benefits, and a life of tranquility.

The upper floor was carpeted as well, with subdued landscapes and portraits from whatever noble family once owned this pile. He made his way to the broad hallway running the length of the east wing and checked the numbers on the doors.

A couple of the doors stood open and Konrad peeked inside as he walked past. In one, a nurse spoon fed some pap to a decrepit old man as he sat in a wheelchair. In another, an old woman lay motionless in bed, hooked up to several machines.

Seeing this gave Konrad a new fear—what if Aunt Frieda was incapacitated? He wanted her to suffer, to know that the end was near. He wanted to see the look of defeat in her eyes when he finally got the upper hand.

He slowed. The sign for Room 207 was just ahead. Its door stood open a crack.

A nurse walked toward him from the far end of the hall. Konrad stopped and pretended to look at the package.

The nurse stopped. "Who are you looking for?"

"Inge Pedersen."

"Room 207."

Konrad nodded a thanks, tucking the package under his arm to waste a moment of time. As he hoped, the nurse began to move down the hallway, intent on whatever task would inadvertently leave Aunt Frieda at Konrad's mercy.

Konrad moved to the door, glanced at the nurse's receding back, and rapped softly at on the door.

"Come in," a familiar voice croaked from within.

Konrad let out a little shiver. After all those years, after she had turned into an old woman, that voice still cut him deep.

He stepped into the room.

It was a spacious bedroom, well-appointed with some old oak furnishings and paintings on the wall.

He recognized all of them. She had brought them from her own home.

The home he hated being sent to. The home that had been a prison for him.

And sitting by the open window, beyond which the leaves of a tree rustled in the morning breeze, sat Aunt Frieda.

She hadn't changed much. Oh, she had aged, that scowling face now deeply seamed with wrinkles. That blonde hair faded to gray so pale as to be almost white. But essentially she remained unchanged. She still had that haughty bearing unbent by the years, and the blue eyes that fixed on him looked ready to pass judgement.

"Hello," Konrad said, standing in the doorway.

"Hello. What do you want?"

"What do you think I want?" Konrad asked, stepping inside the room and closing the door behind him.

"What are you doing?" Aunt Frieda said, surprised.

Konrad blinked. "You don't know who I am, do you?"

"You're a delivery man, and you have the wrong room. No one sends me anything."

“People have to care about you to send you something, you old hag.”

Aunt Frieda leapt out of her chair with surprising energy for one her age.

“How dare you speak like that to me!”

Konrad paced across the room. “I’ll speak to you any way I want, Aunt Frieda.”

Confusion, then recognition. A growing smile revealed yellow teeth.

“Oh, that little loser who I put in his place all those years ago.”

“You’re the loser today.”

Recognition replaced by fear. That made Konrad feel warm inside.

Aunt Frieda ducked to the right, where on the bedside table was a button that probably summoned a nurse.

Konrad cut her off. “Oh no you don’t!”

Aunt Frieda backed away, and the terror on her face made all those years of suffering worth it.

“Go away. I’ll scream!”

“The hall is empty, and that door is thick. No one will hear you. At least not in time.”

“What do you want?”

“You already asked that. Isn’t it obvious?”

Konrad opened the Fedex package and pulled out the garotte. Slowly, so she could see what was in store for her.

Her eyes grew wide.

“No!” Aunt Frieda ran for the window. “Help!”

Konrad rushed over to her, gave her a slap that sent her reeling, and looked out the window. No one stood within a hundred meters except for a withered old man with a walker who probably wouldn’t have heard her if she had been standing right next to him.

Konrad whirled around to see her leaning against one of the bedposts, nursing her reddened cheek.

“Please … please don’t kill me with that.”

“Oooooh, begging now, are we? Looking for mercy, are we? When you never showed it yourself?”

“I-I was sick. A psychological disorder. That’s what they said. Narcissistic personality something. I’m just as much a victim as you.”

Konrad raised an eyebrow. "Being a bitch is a form of victimhood now? Sorry, I can't keep up with the new morality. I'll just kill you instead."

He snapped the garotte tight, the piano wire making a musical hum, and held it close to her face so she could see what she was getting.

And then he reconsidered.

He thought of that camper, that Frenchman with the radio. Konrad had nothing against him, he had simply been in the wrong place at the wrong time. He had to go. Konrad had killed him quickly.

Aunt Frieda didn't deserve to die quickly.

Konrad tossed the garotte aside and reached for her neck with his bare hands.

"Help! Help!"

Aunt Frieda's cries got cut off as Konrad's hands clamped around her neck.

Not too hard, just hard enough to shut her up.

Just hard enough to cut off most of the air and leave her choking and turning red.

She would die slowly. And he would look into those terrified eyes as the life guttered out of them.

Aunt Frieda smacked him, ran her nails down his face, even tried to knee him in the balls. Konrad just stood there and took it. He had endured so much pain from this woman that these blows didn't matter.

All that mattered was looking into those eyes and knowing he had finally won.

The sound of booted feet running down the corridor told him he hadn't won yet.

Tossing Aunt Frieda aside, he spun around in time to see tow gendarmes appear at the doorway. Konrad whipped out a knife and held it to his aunt's throat.

"Back off! Back off of I'll slaughter her like the pig she is."

The gendarmes froze, then took a step back. Konrad held the knife against Aunt Frieda's neck, his hand trembling.

CHAPTER TWENTY SIX

Alexa agonized in the passenger's seat of a French patrol car as the gendarme driving translated the news coming over the police radio. The local police in that rural region could only spare two officers. They had gone to the retirement home and apparently arrived just after Konrad Richter had broken into his aunt's room disguised as a Fedex employee.

When the gendarmes had burst in, Konrad had pulled out a knife and threatened to slash her throat "like my cousin has been practicing to do." The gendarmes had no choice but to back off, and Konrad had locked the door to the room. A standoff had ensued. Backup was on the way, but it appeared Alexa and her crew would make it there first.

Not soon enough, Alexa worried. *That standoff is only for Konrad to gain time. He's trying to think of a way to escape. But he's not going anywhere without his aunt dead first.*

I wish Stuart was driving. We'd already be there by now.

The two police cars carrying them and a couple of gendarmes sped through some beautiful countryside that none of them had time to admire. They pulled up to the open gate of a sprawling old palace and got waved through by an anxious looking security guard. The extensive front lawn with its benches and chairs in the shade was abandoned. No doubt the elderly residents had been evacuated.

They drove up a long driveway and parked next to a gushing fountain. A security guard rushed down the front stairs to meet them.

He started speaking in rapid-fire French and waving his hands in the air as the gendarmes answered back. Frustrated, Alexa stormed up the steps, Stuart and Astrid at her heels.

A nurse who spoke some English led them upstairs, barely keeping up as Alexa bounded up the grand staircase three steps at a time. They got to the top and passed down a broad hallway with numbered doors. A pair of gendarmes and a security guard stood at one of the doors.

After a brief language confusion, they got the security guard speaking English.

"He's still locked in there. He's been shouting in German at Mrs. Pedersen. I don't know what he's saying but at least she's alive. I've heard her cry out."

"Do you have anyone guarding the window?" Alexa asked.

"Yes," the security guard said. "A pair of my colleagues. But it's a long way down. I don't think he'll try to jump if he values his life."

"We don't know that he does," Alexa replied. "Have you tried negotiating with him?"

"He doesn't want to talk other than to warn us off."

Alexa knocked on the door. It felt thick and solid, difficult to break down. "Konrad Richter! I am Deputy U.S. Marshal Alexa Chase. Do you speak English?"

A defiant voice replied, muffled by the oaken door. "Stay away! I'm not giving up in any language."

"We have your cousin Brent in custody. Give yourself up."

"Hunted him all the way from America, did you? I hope he killed plenty before you got him. I only wish he could be here to see this."

Alexa heard the sound of a blow and a woman crying out.

"We need tear gas," Alexa whispered.

"We have none," the gendarme who drove them up said. "And my colleagues here don't have any either. This is a peaceful region. No need for it."

Stuart pulled her away from the door.

"I have an idea," he said in a low voice. "I took a look at the outside wall. It's all big masonry blocks. Plenty of handholds and footholds. I can climb it."

Alexa blinked. "Are you sure?"

"We did some mountaineering training in the Army, not that I got to use it in the Anbar province. And I use a climbing wall at the gym."

"You have ropes in the gym."

"There wasn't a hostage situation at the gym."

Alexa looked at him for a moment, unsure what to say.

"Make some noise," Stuart said. "Talk to him. Make loud demands that he give himself up. The others can make noise too so it sounds like you're preparing something. He'll watch the door and I can get in through the window without him noticing."

"It's a big risk."

Stuart gave her an uncertain smile. "No. Signing up for a second tour of duty was a big risk. Well, more stupid than anything else. Anyway, I don't see any other option."

Alexa looked around at Astrid and the gendarmes. None of them seemed to want to give an opinion.

And she didn't either. This was his choice.

He indicated his choice by running down the hallway.

* * *

Stuart needed to learn to keep his mouth shut. As he looked up at the old stone wall, he had to admit to himself he wasn't sure he could climb it.

He'd exaggerated is climbing skill a bit. Yeah, he'd done some mountaineering training, but no more than any other new recruit in basic training, and that had been ten years ago. At least he'd been on his gym's climbing wall.

Once.

This wall was taller. And as Alexa had so kindly pointed out, there were no ropes.

A tall tree stood nearby, just close enough to be tantalizing and just far enough away to be useless.

An old woman's life was at stake, so he shucked off his jacket, shoes, and socks, and gripped the edge of the highest stone he could reach.

The wall was built of large blocks of masonry, each one carved back a bit at the edges to give it a pleasing pattern. That also allowed for convenient handholds and footholds. As he pulled himself up and got a good foothold, Stuart wondered if the peasants during the French Revolution had climbed up this way.

More likely they had just barged through the front door with pitchforks and torches.

Sometimes angry mobs had it easier than cops. Lucky peasants.

Are you really doing this for Frieda Richter? he asked himself as he clambered up the wall faster than he thought he would. *Or are you doing this for someone else?*

Because he had felt a growing urge to impress Alexa for some time now.

He passed the first floor window and continued up. The second floor window where the assailant and victim were was right above that one, which meant he'd have to climb another ten feet or so and traverse a few more.

His speed began to slow and his confidence began to wane. The rough masonry cut into his hands, and even more into his feet, which were softer and bore most of his weight. He knew enough about climbing not to compensate by putting most of his weight on his arms, because that would fatigue him quicker and might make him slip.

Slip!

As he hauled himself up another course of stone, his right hand broke off a chip. For a crazy second he felt his stomach lurch and his feet scrape against the lower course, ready to slide out and away.

Stuart made a desperate grab with his right hand again, found a good grip, and hung there for a second, trying to catch his breath.

A security guard below him hissed in fright.

He sounded an awful long way down.

Don't think about it. Just think about how much of a rock star you'll look like when you climb in the window and subdue Konrad.

Stuart kept climbing.

He could hear voices now, not far above him and a bit to the right. A male voice shouting in German. Distracted as he was, Stuart couldn't make out the words.

It didn't matter. Alexa and the others were keeping him distracted. That's all Stuart needed.

Actually he needed more than that. The slip and near fall had tensed his muscles and left him exhausted. His fingers and forearms ached, he was pretty sure his feet were bleeding, and his right leg was beginning to scissor, a muscle reaction to fatigue in which it starts pumping up and down. Not the best way to climb a sheer wall.

He put more weight on his left leg, hoping it wouldn't start scissoring too.

The white window frame came into Stuart's peripheral vision. He climbed up another course of stone, that right leg still giving him trouble, and started to edge to the right to get below the window.

The new movement caused him even more trouble. His right leg trembled worse than before, and his left leg began to hint that it wanted to do the same.

Jesus, Stuart. If you were going to fall, couldn't you have done it right at the beginning?

He tried not to think about that, and tried not to think that just below him wasn't a flowerbed or lush lawn, but a gravel path that would hurt like hell if he plunged two stories down onto it.

Or it might not hurt at all. It might be light's out for Stuart Barrett.

Shut up and be a hero. You're doing it for her.

Stuart meant to refer the old woman who he could hear crying out as she got hit yet again, but all his could see in his mind's eye was Alexa's face.

Because she was what he had been looking for all along. A tough woman who knew how to take command in a volatile situation. Someone who spoke her mind and didn't change it every ten seconds like Annette. But also someone with a gentle side, as her concern and obvious hurt about the Stacy situation proved.

There had been a woman in his platoon like that. Corporal Pia Flores. Could gun down terrorists with the best of them and in the next patrol play dolls and hopscotch with the little Iraqi girls. Smart too. Learned more Arabic than anyone else in the platoon.

He'd had a major crush on her. He kept his mouth shut, though. She had a fiancée stateside.

You and your inappropriate desires.

Like your desire to climb a damn wall to impress your partner.

He got right below the window ledge. Konrad was shouting louder now, mostly swear words, working himself up to a fever pitch.

A good thing, too, because Stuart was breathing so hard Konrad would have heard him otherwise.

Someone pounded on the door to keep Konrad facing that direction. Stuart, both legs trembling and his torn up hands barely keeping a grip on the rough stone, made a final effort. He threw up his left hand, felt himself slip, and smacked the hand down on the window ledge. He got a good grip and with the last of his strength hauled himself up.

The room came into view, and the situation looked worse than he had feared. Konrad had a garotte around his aunt Frieda's neck, choking her but not so tightly as to kill her. He was cackling, a broad grin on his face.

And Stuart could see this because Konrad had just turned around to check what the noise from the window was.

Konrad's eyes registered shock, then rage. As Stuart struggled to lift himself up over the windowsill, Konrad tossed Frieda aside like a rag doll, her head impacting with the bed post, and charged at Stuart.

"Now!" Stuart shouted, his voice coming out weak from exhaustion. He didn't think they'd hear on the other side of that heavy door.

Stuart only managed to life himself halfway up when Konrad charged at him with full force, hands outstretched to push him into open air.

CHAPTER TWENTY SEVEN

"Now!"

Stuart's cry was barely audible through the thick wood of the door, but Alexa heard it.

She also heard the fear and desperation in his voice.

Stepping back, she gave the door a hard kick right next to the lock.

It shuddered, but did not break.

She kicked it again, harder this time. A jolt of pain ran up her leg.

Astrid got beside her and, with perfect timing, kicked the door at the same instant Alexa did.

A splintering of wood and the door flung open.

An old woman Alexa assumed to be Frieda was on her knees next to the bed, hands nursing a bleeding bruise on her forehead and gasping for breath. A livid red line ran around the front part of her neck.

Konrad and Stuart struggled at the window. Stuart was halfway out, Konrad trying to push him over. Stuart held onto him with both hands while Konrad swung him back and forth and tried to punch him. Her partner couldn't do anything more than hang on for dear life.

Alexa got across the room like a shot, leaping over Frieda and grabbing Konrad by the shirt. She hauled him back a step, dragging Stuart along with him. He scrambled to get his legs over the windowsill but didn't quite make it before Konrad elbowed Alexa hard in the ribs, making her let go and stagger back.

Konrad ignored her, instead pushing back at Stuart. For a heart-clenching moment it looked like he'd go over, but Stuart managed to hook a leg over and ended up sitting on the windowsill, legs clenched on the wall as if riding a leaping horse. Maybe those lessons at her dad's ranch were entire failures after all.

Alexa wrapped an arm around Konrad's neck and got him into a chokehold.

Almost.

Konrad twisted to the left, slamming her into the wall. Her grip loosened enough that the killer got a strong hand on her forearm and pulled it away enough for him to breathe and move more easily. Stuart gripped Konrad by the shirt front, while one of the gendarmes suddenly appeared and gave Konrad a nice jab in the face.

But it didn't make Konrad give up.

With a snarl he pressed the palm of his free hand into Stuart's chin, pushing his head back and making him lean out the window. Stuart kept a grip on Konrad's shirt. The gendarme clocked Konrad another one in the nose, making it spout blood. The killer didn't seem to notice, all his will intent on killing the lawman who had climbed through the window.

Alexa pulled him back, hoping to pull Stuart with him.

A tearing sound as the fabric of Konrad's shirt parted. Stuart tottered on the edge and began to fall out, arms cartwheeling, tipping over as if in slow motion.

Alexa and the gendarme both reached for him and only ended up getting in each other's way. Stuart toppled over the edge.

Desperate, Alexa lunged for him, grabbing him by one ankle, but the force of his fall nearly took her over the edge too. She ended up draped over the windowsill, the wooden frame digging into her stomach, gripping her upside down partner, feeling her hold loosen until the gendarme grabbed Stuart's other leg.

For a moment, everyone forgot about Konrad Richter.

Until, that is, Alexa felt him grab her leg and lift it.

A moment before she lost her balance and went over the edge, she heard the unmistakable sound of a truncheon hitting flesh.

"Schweinhund!" Astrid shouted. Another thud against flesh. Konrad let go.

Alexa and the gendarme hauled Stuart up and into the window like fishermen hauling a tuna into their boat. He ended up on a heap on the floor.

Alexa turned and found Astrid smacking Konrad for all she was worth. The warm feeling that gave Alexa in the pit of her stomach should have troubled her, but didn't. Not at all.

But Konrad wasn't out of the fight yet. He leapt up, belting Astrid across the jaw, and shoved her toward the window. She lost her balance and stumbled toward the open space.

He's trying to kill one last blonde woman, Alexa realized.

Alexa and the gendarme rushed for him, the gendarme slightly behind because he had to get around Stuart, who was still trying to pick himself off the floor. It was up to Alexa.

She grabbed Astrid and yanked her out of Konrad's grasp. The killer's forward momentum made him smash against the window, topple over, and in an instant he was gone.

Both woman poked their heads out the window and looked down. Konrad lay on the gravel walkway below, his neck at a sharp angle. Dead.

"You saved my life," Astrid said, panting. "Thank you."

"And you saved mine," Stuart said. He put a hand on Alexa's shoulder. "Both of you."

They turned to where Frieda Richter sat at the edge of the bed. She was a mess, with an ugly wound along her neck and bruises all around her head and arms.

"Don't worry, Mrs. Richter," Alexa said. "Konrad's dead. He can't hurt you anymore."

Her eyes widened. "He died from the fall?"

"Yes. He broke his neck."

Frieda burst out laughing. "That's hilarious! He tried to push you out and fell out himself. What a moron! What a loser! He always was useless, him and my son!"

She kept on laughing while law enforcement officials from three countries looked on in horror.

* * *

The gendarmes took over the crime scene, interviewing everyone and taking photos of the room and Konrad's body. Astrid and Stuart helped, giving statements to the local police for their reports.

Alexa bowed out of all of it. She felt utterly spent. Finished. She sat in an antique gilded chair with a red velvet cushion, holding a coffee a nurse had put in her hand.

The long chase, the hunt across three nations, the string of dead bodies, all of it overwhelmed her, but not as much as that evil old woman cackling at the death of her nephew, and the second bout of laughter when she heard about the incarceration of her son.

That's what bad parenting does to kids, Alexa thought.

Of course not all abused and neglected children turn into serial killers. They all get marked, though. Substance abuse, depression, anger issues, a whole host of mental and emotional and social problems.

Like falling for a seventeen-year-old when you're only thirteen. Or running away to camp out in the middle of the desert.

Alexa grimaced. Stacy was heading down a bad road, and Alexa didn't know what she could do to stop her.

Because Alexa simply didn't have the time to give her the attention she needed and deserved. This was the second case in as many months that had taken her overseas. While coming to Europe was unusual, she felt sure that more cases would take her south of the border. The nature of crime in Arizona made it all too common.

But at least this case was done, despite the bitter and unsatisfying as the result. Frieda Richter belonged in jail right next to her son.

Alexa checked her phone. Still no message from Stacy. Stuart hadn't heard anything either. He would have mentioned it.

Alexa sent her a text. "Case closed. Coming home in a day or two. How are Smith and Wesson?"

She pressed send. Trying to calculate the time in Arizona, she figured Stacy would probably see it. She often stayed up late texting and watching YouTube, like everyone in her generation. It wasn't like she had parents to tell her to go to sleep at a decent hour. Hell, half the time they kept her up.

Maybe she was staying at the ranch, getting a bit of peace. Or would her days-long sulk keep her from doing that?

Alexa stared at her phone. No response. Granted, it had only been thirty seconds, but if the kid was up she'd respond immediately. Assuming she wanted to respond.

Assuming she'd ever respond ever again.

Don't be ridiculous. She's a kid in a sulk.

Nevertheless, Alexa found herself writing another text.

"I'm not feeling good right now and it would really help if I heard from you."

She sent the text, then stared at her phone. What kind of a message was that for an adult to send to a kid? Stacy wasn't her friend. She was family. Sort of. She was supposed to rely on Alexa for emotional support, not the other way around.

Although now that she thought about it, Alexa realized that she needed the kid as much as the kid needed her.

Because what else did she have in her life? A few close friends she didn't get to see often enough. A rocky relationship with a family she didn't get to see enough. And a partner who had been acting weird ever since he got dumped. Stacy had become an important part of her life, right up there with her career. And now she wouldn't even reply to her texts unless Stuart told her to.

As the gendarmes bustled back and forth, taking photos and statements, and as the body of Konrad Richter got taken away to the morgue, and as Frieda Richter got taken away to a hospital to have her wounds treated, Alexa sat in the hallway of an old French palace, unaware of the activity, or of the luxury and history surrounding her, staring at a phone that remained agonizingly silent.

CHAPTER TWENTY EIGHT

Alexa didn't get a message that day, or the morning after before as they went to the airport to board a plane back to the United States. Astrid saw them to Charles De Gaulle airport, along with one of the homicide detectives.

"You have performed a great service for France," the homicide detective announced, shaking their hands. "You are welcome in Paris any time."

"Hopefully in better circumstances," Alexa said.

"Not a bad place to have a vacation," Stuart said, turning to Alexa. "Maybe we should take him up on it."

Alexa gave him an awkward smile and turned to Astrid.

"Thank you for all your help. We couldn't have done it without you."

Astrid grinned. "Yes, you could have. You make a great team. Don't let anyone break it up."

Alexa and Stuart glanced at each other and Stuart shot her a warm smile. The call for boarding came over the P.A. system.

"Let's go," Alexa said. She couldn't decide if she was glad to be returning to the States, or dreading it.

"I had a word with the crew," the gendarme said, nudging Stuart with his elbow. "You've been bumped to first class."

"That's our first bit of good news in a long time," Alexa said. "Thank you."

After a final round of handshakes, they went to the front of the line and got ushered to a pair of spacious adjoining seats right at the front of the plane. Before she had to put her phone on flight mode, she took a video and sent it to Stacy.

"Flying like a rock star!" she wrote.

It didn't make her feel better. The kid probably wouldn't respond to this message either.

"Did you hear from Stacy?" she asked Stuart, who was also looking at his phone.

"Hold on, I was checking some work texts," Stuart said. Alexa felt a spike of embarrassment. She was obsessing too much about this, she knew, and yet she couldn't help it. "Um, yeah! Here."

He turned his phone to show a photo of Smith and Wesson, freshly curried, standing in the corral.

The warmth that brought to Alexa's heart quickly cooled. Why hadn't Stacy sent her that too?

Her feelings must have been apparent on her face because Stuart said, "Don't worry. This is a signal to you. She's never sent me a photo of the horses before, except for one embarrassing one of me getting trying to mount one of your dad's horses the wrong way. Actually, she's sent me more texts on this trip than she's ever done since I met her. This isn't for me. This is for you. She knows I'll show them to you."

"So she's telling me she doesn't want to talk to me," Alexa grumbled.

"She'll cool down. This time tomorrow, you'll be back on your little ranch outside of Phoenix where she wants you to be."

"Until next time," Alexa said.

Stuart sighed. "Until next time, yes."

The plane took off. Alexa settled in her seat, which she discovered could extend into a bed, complete with a low partition to afford some privacy, or at least as much as one could expect on an airplane.

Alexa had never flown first class, most federal agencies were so cheap they'd strap their agents to the wings if they could get away with it, so she wasn't expecting the champagne that came once they had leveled off at 33,000 feet.

While she had never been much of a drinker, and she'd heard that alcohol was bad for jetlag, some champagne sounded good right at that moment. They were off duty, after all, and they'd managed to stop two serial killers.

"To a brilliant partnership," Stuart said, clinking his glass against hers.

Or at least trying to clink them. They turned out to be plastic. Alexa and Stuart shared a chuckle.

"So … " Stuart said, looking at her over the rim of his glass. "What's next for the dynamic duo?"

"Who knows? I'm sure they'll throw something at us. We never get to rest for long."

"And that's the way you like it."

"Ugh. Everyone tells me I work too hard."

"Allow me to add my voice to the chorus."

"It's not like you're a slacker."

"Touché, as the gendarmes would say. Did you see that guy slugging Konrad? I'm surprised he didn't knock him out."

"Konrad had a lifetime of fury built up inside him. A few punches wouldn't stop him."

A lifetime of fury based on a miserable childhood. I wonder what Frieda did to them?

God, what's going to happen to Stacy?

"You're thinking about Stacy again, and how her crap parents are going to screw her up."

Alexa blinked. "Are you a mind reader now?"

"I think I know you pretty well by this point."

Alexa shifted in her seat. "Well, partners see the best and worst of each other."

"I'm mostly seeing the best," Stuart said, staring at her.

Okaaaay.

"So have you heard from Annette?" she asked.

Stuart's face darkened. She didn't like hurting him like this, but she didn't want the conversation turning down the path he seemed to want it to go.

And that made her feel … strange. What was that feeling? Regret? Did he want him to go down that path? Did she like the attention, even if it was inappropriate?

Because she had been thinking a lot about him lately, and not all of those thoughts were related to work.

"She hasn't gotten in touch," he mumbled into his champagne glass.

The satisfaction that gave her felt more than a little unsettling. It was unfair to him, and raised too many questions about herself.

"Give her a chance," Alexa forced herself to say. "She'll come around in time. I think you two are good for each other."

That was an outright lie. Alexa didn't think Annette would come around in time, and she didn't think they were good for each other, for exactly the reasons Annette had spelled out.

"I'm going to get some sleep," Stuart said. He put up the partition.

Alexa put up hers too. They spoke little for the rest of the flight.

* * *

"This did not go well," the senator grumbled.

"They solved it too quickly," the FBI man said. "I didn't have time to put anything in place!"

"Now instead of them being national heroes, they're international heroes," the senator snapped. "My overseas contacts say both the Germans and the French are talking about giving them commendations."

"Can you stop it?" the FBI man asked, sounding fearful.

"My colleague in Germany can probably quash that one. The French commendation will probably get lost in their own bureaucracy."

"Good. That's good."

"No, that's only less bad," the senator snapped. "We still have them getting applauded by both the FBI and the U.S. Marshals service. And the way things are going, we can't keep this out of the national news for long. It already made national news in Germany and France, naming their names too."

"Jesus. It's only a matter of time before they get their own agency. All this time establishing control, and now this happens. What are we going to do?"

Both men paused, waiting for an answer.

A feeble old voice came on the line, carrying the heavy weight of authority.

"We need to stop this. Now."

"How?" the FBI man said, his voice breaking.

"We have to break up this partnership. It's too late to trip them up in the field, so we need to attack them from a personal angle. Dig into their pasts, and check out their present as well. Everyone has secrets. Find out what they are and use those to break them apart. I want their reputations destroyed and their partnership terminated, *before* they get another case. Get to work on this, people. Enough fooling around. I want results and I want them now."

The FBI man, sounding even more nervous than before, replied, "But sir, as I said before, character assassination can backfire. If we—"

"Results. Now. Get to it."

"Yes, sir," the FBI man and the senator said.

Three electronic beeps sounded over the line and the man in charge hung up.

CHAPTER TWENTY NINE

Alexa drove down the darkened country highway north of Phoenix, her eyelids heavy. They had landed in Phoenix in the afternoon, and had to go to a debriefing with Marshal Hernandez. He offered to put it off to the next day, but they had decided to get it over with and take a couple of well-earned days off.

And if Alexa were to be honest, she had been happy to put off coming home, because then she'd have to deal with all that entailed. Stacy still hadn't texted her.

The afternoon hadn't been all bad. They'd received a standing ovation when they entered the U.S. Marshals office, and a call from Stuart's boss in D.C., Deputy Director Sandford.

"I'm working with Hernandez to make this collaboration permanent," he told them. "We need to get it cleared through Congress in the next budget debates, but given your batting average I'm going to be able to line up a bunch of members of both houses to add you as a rider to next year's budget. That means a dedicated office and support staff. In the meantime, keep doing what you're doing and I think we'll get over any objections."

"What objections could there be at this point?" Alexa asked Stuart once they got off the phone. "We've caught every criminal we've been sent after."

Stuart gave her a high five, his bad mood on the flight washed away as they bathed in praise.

"Oh, he I think he was worried about the Washington bean counters. Clear sailing from here on in."

At last, after they finished all the paperwork, Stuart had suggested a celebratory beer.

"Oh, I don't think so," Alexa had said, noting the disappointment in his face. "If I had a drink I think I'd end up falling asleep at the bar."

He gave her a tight smile. "Not a good look for an officer of the law. OK. See in you in a couple of days."

While the excuse was true enough, that wasn't why she had made it. Stuart had shown obvious interest in her ever since getting dumped by Annette. Totally inappropriate and a really bad idea for the both of them. She didn't want to be Rebound Woman, and Stuart sure didn't need that either. Better to cold shoulder him and hope he got the message.

Except, and she had finally admitted this to herself, she didn't want to cold shoulder him. He had a lot of noble qualities, qualities that a social butterfly like Annette couldn't appreciate. Oh, she could see them well enough, and that's what drove her off. Stuart had too much potential as a long-term partner, and that scared the crap out of Annette.

It scared the crap out of Alexa too. She shouldn't have these feelings for a man who was her partner, and yet there they were.

She'd keep those feelings under control, however, because even if it didn't constitute workplace impropriety, she would still be Rebound Woman, and she sure as hell didn't want to play that role.

That perfectly valid excuse to avoid her feelings came as a profound relief.

So now she drove alone down the familiar back country road, windows open to catch the warm desert air. Her ranch-style home appeared in the darkness up ahead, the porch light on as it always was. The lights were on in the Carpenter trailer in the distance off to the right. For once she didn't hear loud music and drunken bawling. Maybe her neighbors had partied early and were sleeping it off.

Her heart sunk as she pulled into the drive and didn't see any more lights on in her house.

Wait. She caught a faint glimmering through the living room curtains, as of a phone being switched off. Stacy must be in there texting. Alexa had told that girl a million times not to stare at her phone in the dark.

"You only get one set of eyes," she'd say, as Stacy rolled hers.

Smiling, Alexa parked her Jeep and got out. So Stacy had decided to stay over the night she got back. Good. Hopefully she hadn't had to wait too long.

As Alexa walked up to her front door, she felt a pang of worry. Why had she turned her phone off? Certainly not to follow the old injunction to spare her eyes. Was she sneaking out the back door, intent on continuing her sulk? No, probably not. Knowing her, she was probably going to break the tension with a surprise, like when she had put balloons all over the place and that banner. Or maybe she'd jump out of the shadows and scare her. She'd done that once when she was younger. Alexa had almost pulled a gun on her.

Well, two could play at the surprise game. Suppressing her joy, and her itchy trigger finger, Alexa quietly unlocked the door. Then she waited a moment. She let it stretch out, barely able to keep from laughing.

After enough time to catch Stacy off guard, she burst the door open, shouting, "BOO!"

A shadow jerked just to the left, then rushed for her.

"St—"

It only took an instant to realize this was not who she wanted to see. This was someone else.

And that instant nearly cost Alexa her life.

A man, short and slim but moving with the speed and grace of a panther, rushed her, a knife gleaming in the porch light's shine.

Alexa leapt backwards, trying to get out the door, knowing she was too late, and in her rush slamming a shoulder into the doorjamb.

A hot pain slashed across her midriff as the knife intended on gutting her only sliced her flesh.

It was just a graze, but enough to make her jerk with pain and surprise. Her attacker raised his knife to slash down at her face.

Quick as lightning, she grabbed his wrist with both hands and tried to knee him in the balls. Her assailant turned his body, her knee impacting with his thigh. He kept the twist going, extending a leg and pulling his arm down to trip her up.

She ended up getting flipped and landing on the floor.

Alexa turned that fall into a roll, the knife scraping against the wooden floor where her throat had been a moment before.

She kept rolling until the couch and coffee table stopped her. The man dove for her, quick as an eyeblink, and Alexa, helpless on her back, could only grab the coffee table and lift it over herself as a shield.

The knife thunked into the wood. Alexa smashed it into the intruder, making him back up a step.

She tried to rise, her improvised shield slipped and the knife slashing so close to her head she felt sure she lost some hair.

As her attacker came in for a backhand, she managed to get to one knee and bring up the coffee table again. The knife scraped against the wood a second time. Then the table bucked, smashing against her face and body Alexa found herself on the floor.

He had kicked it. He kicked again, knocking it aside with a clatter.

Alexa scrambled backwards like a crab. Her hand came down on something and on instinct she threw it. Nothing but the TV remote. It smacked into the guy's face and didn't slow him down at all. He dove in, leading with his knife.

Alexa kicked his hand, and by some miracle didn't get cut. The keen blade ran along the strong leather of her cowboy boot.

The boot of her other foot landed squarely on his shin.

He let out a grunt and fell hard to his knees, letting out another cry of pain from the impact. Alexa pulled back both legs and kicked out, feeling a nick as the knife grazed her calf. The man flew back, falling on his back.

Alexa scrambled to her feet, pulling out her gun.

Just as she flicked off the safety, the knife flew through the air, slashing at the back of her hand and making her drop her weapon.

The intruder came next, arms wide to grab her in a tackle.

They both went down in a tangle of flailing limbs. Alexa gave him a good one on the side of the head and he did the same to her.

Alexa struggled to get on top, but the pain from three cuts and the man's fearsome strength made it a losing battle. After a few seconds of struggle, he ended up straddling her …

… and pulled out a second knife.

It was tucked in a sheath in the small of his back, and getting it out took a precious second, one that Alexa didn't waste. She wrenched her body to the left, rocking the man on top of her but not managing to throw him off.

She didn't think she would, but it did give her room to draw her nightstick.

Alexa had no room and no time to swing, so she jabbed it up at him.

The tip caught him in the soft flesh between the jaw and the throat. He made a strangled, gulping sound and teetered back.

Now Alexa did have room and time to swing, and she swung for all she was worth.

The nightstick made a satisfying crack on the side of his skull and he toppled to the side.

Alexa rolled away, ran into the couch, and struggled to rise.

By the time she did, the man was on his hands and knees, grabbing his knife.

Alexa swung low, hitting him in the back of the elbow. The snap of bone, the flash of the knife flying away into the shadows, and the intruder made a faceplant into Alexa's floor.

She hit him again on the back of the head, then kicked him to roll him over. While that brought a twinge of pain from the cut on her calf, she had far too much adrenaline pumping through her system to care.

Alexa looked around for her gun and didn't spot it. The living room only had the faint light of the porch coming in through the open front door and the white curtains.

A slight movement at her feet made her look down again. Her attacker had shifted, and now lay perfectly still once more.

He's faking it. He's not unconscious.

Alexa jabbed the end of her nightstick hard into his stomach. His legs and arms shot up as he let out a cry.

"Who sent you?" she demanded.

He was coughing and gasping too much to answer.

Then another thought came to her.

She'd had been away for four days. How long had he been hiding here? Stacy had been feeding the horses, which meant …

"Stacy!" she shouted.

The darkened house gave no answer.

"Stacy!"

The assailant gasped, clutching his stomach with his one good arm, the other lying useless and bent the wrong way. Even so, he managed a laugh.

"Is that the little girlie who comes and feeds the horses?"

"What did you do to her?" Alexa demanded.

"I've been waiting here two days. Had to do something to pass the time."

"You bastard!"

He laughed, then his one good hand shot out. Alexa saw the vague form of the knife lying in the shadow of the overturned coffee table. She brought her nightstick down on his hand, the small bones crumpling under the force of her blow.

"Ah!"

Alexa straddled him, her knee grinding into his ruined hand.

"Where is she? What did you do?"

He gasped and panted, little bursts of laughter making it through the pain.

"What did you do to her?"

With a snarl, she cast aside her nightstick and grabbed the knife. Clenching his injured jaw in one hand, she held up the knife to his face.

"Tell me!"

His grin caught the light from the porch, making him look like some evil apparition materializing out of the shadows.

"See that chip off the tip of the blade? That's when it cut through her vertebrae."

With an enraged roar, Alexa raised the knife. Just then he headbutted her.

Alexa's head felt like it was at the center of an explosion. For a moment she blacked out, and by the time she came to, the killer had struggled to his feet. He had a shattered hand and a broken elbow, but that didn't stop him from attacking.

With a cackle, he landed a hard kick to her side. Alexa grunted, the force of the impact actually pushing her a couple of feet.

Another kick followed the first. Alexa scrabbled around in the shadows until her hand clasped the knife.

When he tried to kick her a third time, his leg got skewered by his own blade.

The killer let out a howl and fell. Alexa swarmed over him, stabbing, jabbing that knife into his gut again and again and again.

She didn't stop until long after he was dead.

Alexa stumbled away, drenched in blood, sickened at what he had said, sickened with the image of Stacy suffering, and most of all sickened with herself.

She had acted like Konrad, like Brent. She had acted like the person Drake Logan had always said she was.

An animal. A killer.

But he hurt Stacy.

No excuse. You're an officer of the law.

Stacy …

With a sense of dread, she stumbled over to the hallway and switched on the light. Alexa glanced around the living room but didn't see Stacy there. She tried not to look at the leaking mess on her floor that had once been a man.

"Stacy!"

Her wounds were starting to sting now, and she felt her uniform dampen from both the blood flowing from them and the sweat gushing out every pore.

CHAPTER THIRTY

"Stacy!"

Alexa burst into the guest room, Stacy's room, and found the bed neatly made and everything in order. Alexa checked the bathroom. Nothing. With a sense of dread she checked the master bedroom.

The bed was unmade and had obviously been slept in. The killer had spoken the truth. He had spent the night here. But she didn't see Stacy, or any sign she had been here.

She ran to the kitchen, found nothing, and burst out the back door.

"Stacy!"

Maybe he killed her and put her in the stable.

"Stacy!"

One of the horses whinnied. Why? Fear from her voice, or because of a body in the stable? Horses were afraid of dead bodies …

"Oh my God, Stacy!"

"What the hell's going on over there?"

That came from the Carpenter trailer. She turned and saw Mr. Carpenter, in a t-shirt and underwear, standing in front of the trailer, shotgun in hand.

"I can't find Stacy!"

"She's over here. You think your ranch is her permanent address? What's the matter with you?"

"Is she all right?"

"Yeah. Why wouldn't she be?"

Alexa fell to her knees and sobbed with relief. Mr. Carpenter came running over.

"There's been another attack, hasn't there?"

He made it sound like an accusation, and in Alexa's heart, she couldn't disagree.

* * *

The doctor released her in the early hours of the morning. Stuart and Marshal Hernandez were in the hospital waiting room when she came out stiff with stitches and groggy from painkillers.

"We've got you a motel for the night," her boss said. "Annette is still documenting the crime scene and … cleaning up."

Both men looked uncomfortable. When Annette had arrived, an expert who had seen everything in her time at CSI, she had given her a look of shock.

I tore him apart, was the only thought that kept running through Alexa's head. *I stabbed him so much I actually tore him apart.*

And all that would be meticulously documented in reports and photographs and crime scene sketches. The unnecessarily large number of stab wounds, the shattered hand, the broken elbow. Annette would discover, if she hadn't already, that the breaks had come before the stabs. That Alexa hadn't needed to kill him at all.

Of course she wouldn't get in trouble. The man had a criminal record as long as Alexa's arm, and had broken into the private residence of an officer of the law with the intention of murdering her. His death would be ruled self-defense. There would be no trial. There wouldn't even be much of an internal review.

But Annette knew the truth. And so did Stuart. And so did Marshal Hernandez. And so did Captain Filipe Santos, the local lawman who first responded to Alexa's 911 call.

And so would a couple of dozen other people from the local P.D., U.S. Marshals service, and the CSI.

They had all seen grisly evidence that Alexa had darkness inside her. Just as she always feared. Just as Drake Logan always knew.

He knows me better than everybody else. He always said so, and I never believed it.

Sitting in the back seat as Stuart and Marshal Hernandez drove her to a motel, Alexa numbly checked her phone. A missed call from Melanie. That ambulance chaser must have been monitoring police communications and recognized the address. She ignored that. More welcome was the text from Stacy.

"Are you OK?"

"I'm fine. Don't come over. I'm not staying at home tonight."

And I'm not sure I'm worthy of your company.

Stacy replied almost instantly, despite the fact that she had to get up for school in a couple of hours.

"There's like a billion cops over there. Dad has been sitting up all night in front of the trailer with a shotgun."

"You never saw anything when you came to feed Smith and Wesson?"

"No. A policewoman came and asked us that. Was that creep there when I came over?"

Alexa hesitated. She didn't want to lie and she didn't want to tell the truth.

"I don't know."

"God, I hope not."

"I'm staying at a motel tonight. Get some sleep."

"OK. I'll text you in the morning. Are you sure you're not hurt?"

"Not badly. Don't worry about it."

"You sure?"

"I'm sure."

Now I really am lying.

"OK. Love you."

"I love you too, Stacy."

She put away her phone and leaned back in the seat, closing her eyes. Patching things up with Stacy didn't help he mood. She still felt dirty inside.

"We're making a request to have Logan changed to another wing," Marshal Hernandez said as he drove. "It's obvious that there's a leak somewhere, if he was able to order a hit on you. We'll find who passed on the message and there will be hell to pay."

Assuming it even was him. It could have been the Jersey Devil. He's got his eye on me as well.

Why the hell did I ever visit either of them?

Because they're like you.

Alexa shuddered.

"It's going to be all right," Stuart said.

Alexa said nothing.

"I checked on the Carpenters," he went on. "They didn't hear or see anything. It appears your attacker hid in your house and didn't try to interfere with Stacy when she came over to feed the horses."

Alexa nodded. That made sense. He didn't want to risk getting detected when he lay in wait for Alexa.

But he probably watched her from the windows, thinking his thoughts.

And what if she had come into the house?

Alexa shuddered again, and the shuddering didn't stop for a long time.

* * *

The next day, Alexa slept in so late that she didn't get back to the ranch to see Stacy go off to school. She hesitated about reentering her own home, but decided it would be better to mentally reclaim her territory.

Annette and her team had done their job well. The living room was spotless, although they couldn't hide the scrapes on the floor from her assailant's knife, nor the broken lamp and coffee table. There was a slash through the couch too. She hadn't remembered that happening, although the whole evening was a bit of a blur.

She fixed herself a large lunch, creaking around the kitchen, every muscle aching. Once finished, she took a long, hot bath to ease the pain of the bruises the attacker had given her.

After that she did nothing else, because there was nothing else to do.

She hated days off. They made her feel so useless.

At least she had the horses to keep her company. She fed Smith and Wesson, and let them have the run of the corral. But she didn't take them out for a ride. She didn't have the energy.

For a time she listened to the police scanner, picking up all the usual chatter of policework in this semirural area north of Phoenix. She heard Captain Santos respond to a burglary, and his men deal with the usual incidents of drunk driving, speeding, and domestic disturbances. Routine stuff. After a while, she switched the radio off.

Then she sat in her living room. She tried to read a novel and cast it aside. She switched on the daytime news and watched it without really focusing on it. She made herself lunch and ate without really tasting it.

And all the while, she checked her phone. Regular messages from Stacy. Alexa replied, while feeling strangely distant. She had mutilated that man because she thought he'd hurt her, but that didn't forgive what she'd done.

She also got a message from Doctor Brennan, her psychologist. Alexa ignored it. She ignored the second message too.

Maybe I can go to work tomorrow. Hernandez will understand. Or maybe he won't. But a lecture from him is better than another day of this.

Her doorbell rang.

Alexa grabbed her gun and ducked down, out of sight of the windows and out of the line of fire of the door. She'd had people shoot at her through doors before. Not the best way to hit someone, but a spray of fire could get her easily enough.

From behind the armchair, gun leveled, she called out, "Who is it!"

"It's me, you're neighbor."

That was Mr. Carpenter's voice.

"Are you alone?" Alexa demanded.

"Yeah," he sounded confused, then added, "Oh right, yeah. It's safe. I'm alone."

Even so, Alexa crawled over to the window and peeked over the windowsill, only showing just enough of her head to see out.

Mr. Carpenter stood on her front porch. Alone and seemingly at ease. He did not look like someone being given commands at gunpoint.

Alexa let out a gust of relief, stood, and holstered her gun. She hesitated, then pulled out her gun again.

When she opened the door, she kept to one side.

"Hi," Mr. Carpenter said.

"Hi." Alexa looked around. The area seemed clear.

"A bit jumpy? Well, I can't blame you."

Alexa holstered her weapon and finally focused on him. To her surprise, he looked sober. He even wore a clean shirt and had shaved and had a haircut recently.

"What happened to you?" she blurted. As soon as she said it, she realized how rude that sounded.

Her neighbor only laughed, touching his brand new shirt. Sure, it was just a t-shirt, but it was clean and didn't have pizza stains on it.

"Looking good, eh? I got a job."

Alexa nodded. "That's great."

He'd work sometimes when money got tight, but it never lasted. He'd either get fired for not showing up, or for being late every day for a week, or quit in a huff when a supervisor criticized him.

"Working in a warehouse for a furniture company. Loading trucks, taking stock, that sort of stuff. Ten bucks an hour. They're training me to use the forklift. Once I get the hang of it I'll go up to twelve bucks fifty an hour."

"Sounds like a good job. It's hard to get decent work these days," Alexa said, wondering where this conversation was going.

Mr. Carpenter paused for a moment, looking uncomfortable. "I was wondering if you plan on moving."

"Moving? Hell, no! This is my home. I'm not letting that psycho drive me out."

Whichever psycho that might be.

Her neighbor nodded. "I can respect that. Would be a pain finding a place for your horses too. In that case, I was wondering if you could lend me some money."

Alexa blinked. "Lend you some money?"

Her neighbor raised a hand and hurried to continue. "Just until next payday. I need a down payment on an apartment we've been looking at."

"An apartment?"

"Closer into town. It's a hell of a commute to the warehouse and with gas prices these days … well, and to be honest, it's not safe here. I got my family to think about."

Since when?

"I just need four hundred dollars. I don't know who else to ask. We need to get out of here."

"You're moving away?" Alexa said, the truth of his words finally sinking in.

"This is the second time this has happened. The cops said that creep was even in the house when Stacy came over. What if she'd gone inside? I'm not blaming you, but you got Drake Logan gunning for you, and he's got a whole following of crazies. Sooner or later, another psycho is going to come sneaking around here. What if he grabs Stacy? I can't let that happen. So … I'm giving us all a new start. Got a job, and I haven't had a drop for three days. Well, two days, but I won't drink anything today either. We gotta make a clean break and get set up right."

"By moving away." Alexa looked at her feet.

"It's too dangerous here. Even if I was alone I'd think of leaving. But with a wife and kid to think about … "

He made a helpless gesture.

Alexa sighed. He was right, of course. And he was finally showing some responsibility. Maybe it would even stick this time. Probably not, but maybe. Maybe having murderers prowling around the neighbor's house had woken him up to the fact that he needed to get a job, make money, and live somewhere safer.

I tried to give her a safe space, but that space isn't safe anymore.

Her eyes filled, and despite wanting to hold back, despite not wanting to lose it in front of this annoying and disappointing man, she found herself crying.

"Whoa! Hey. It'll be OK. She can come over once it's safe again. She loves hanging out with you."

"Really?" Alexa sniffled, wiping her eyes.

"Sure. Look, I know we haven't always seen eye to eye, but you're like a favorite aunt or something. I wouldn't take that from her. Once you get all this craziness squared away she can come up on the bus, or you can pick her up. But I got to make sure it's safe first. I mean, she was feeding those horses while that killer was hiding in your house!"

Alexa had nothing to say to that.

Mr. Carpenter gave her a reassuring smile. That caught her by surprise. He'd been nothing but suspicious, guarded, and mildly hostile ever since they'd met.

"She's stuck to you. Oh hey, I got an idea! Maybe you can ride away from the house a couple of miles and meet up with her. I'll drive her to whatever spot you pick. That would be safe."

Is he actually trying to help?

"Got to keep the kid happy," he added, looking a bit embarrassed.

Alexa stared at this mess of a man, and realized he really was trying this time. He had finally realized what his trashy lifestyle was doing to his child and he wanted to make a new start. And now, for the first time, she found herself truly hoping he'd make it.

Because Alexa had always harbored a secret satisfaction that Stacy's parents never looked like they'd change. It gave her a role in the girl's life.

An unworthy emotion, and unfair to Stacy, but she couldn't help her feelings.

"Yeah, maybe we could do that," she said in a small voice.

Mr. Carpenter let out a little laugh. "She'll insist. She showed us those selfies of you feeding the horses in Europe."

Alexa paused. So Stacy hadn't mentioned their argument? She had even shown them the photos without mentioning that Stuart had actually taken them? What was all that about?

Teenagers are from a different planet, one of her coworkers once joked. *Don't try to understand them.*

Turns out that was correct.

The two neighbors fell into silence for a moment. Mr. Carpenter faced her an expectant look in his eye. Alexa realized an unanswered question still hung in the air.

"I'll lend you the money," she said.

"Gee, that means a lot."

"I'll go to the ATM today and get it."

"Sorry I had to ask. But it's the best way."

"It's the only way," Alexa said and sighed. "But could you do me a favor?"

"Sure. Anything."

"Don't tell Stacy I lent you the money."

"Um, all right. That's kinda better anyway. It's a bit awkward."

You mean it makes you look bad, like you're not a provider. Well, I'm giving you a chance to become that. But I don't want you telling her because I don't want her thinking I'm pushing her away.

Mr. Carpenter extended a hand. Alexa shook it.

"So … when will you move?"

"If I get the lease squared away, we can move in by the end of the week. Landlord's gonna fumigate for cockroaches first."

"Right."

Alexa hoped that was only routine. Cockroaches were a big problem in Arizona, and not just in the poorly kept places. Alexa had roach traps scattered all around the house. Most people did.

"I'll come tonight to pick up the money. I really appreciate this, and I'll get it back to you as soon as I can."

"No rush."

"Yeah, there is. I don't like owing people anything, and I owe you enough already. All of us do."

Alexa felt her eyes welling up again.

"Thank you."

"I'll see you soon. Stay safe."

"I'll try."

Mr. Carpenter walked off, heading across the stretch of open desert between Alexa's house and his trailer, taking the path between the two properties that Stacy had worn clear by her daily visits for the past year and a half.

A path she'd never walk again.

EPILOGUE

"We've found an opening," the FBI man said, his voice sounding eager to please.

"Excellent! What is it?" the senator asked.

"The latest attack. Our source told me Alexa went berserk, tearing apart her attacker's insides with a knife."

"A convicted felon who broke into her house with the intent of murdering her? Who cares?"

"It's more than that," the FBI man crowed. "She had already incapacitated him before killing him."

"There'll be plausible deniability, and the public still won't care."

"I'm not done yet," the FBI man said, sounding more confident than ever. "She went to see Drake Logan and the Jersey Devil without permission."

There was a pause on the line. After a moment, the senator spoke, sounding contemplative.

"Hmm, so we could use the psychological angle. She's been affected by her work too much. Got too deep into the heads of killers. Oh, not her fault of course, but she needs to be relieved of duty. Put on health leave for an indeterminate period. For her own good, naturally. Commendation and all that. But with her gone, your man will have no partner. The collaboration will break apart."

"Not necessarily," an old voice croaked.

"What do you think we should do, sir?" the senator asked.

"The U.S. Marshals might try to replace her and keep the collaboration going. We need to paint Stuart Barrett with the same brush."

"I could fake some phone calls showing he knew of the unauthorized visits," the FBI man said, "plus he had an affair with a CSI expert in Phoenix. Although she's not technically a coworker, it doesn't look good."

"We need more," the old man said, his voice fading.

Three loud electronic beeps came over the line.

"Sir?" the senator asked.

"Sir, are you all right?" the FBI man asked.

They heard some choking, then a cough, and the old man's voice came back on the line, sounding twice as determined.

"Get the sister-in-law on board. She's aching to make it to the national level. I'll pull strings with our people in the media to make that happen. She can break a story about how both Chase and Barrett were giving favors to serial killers to satisfy their lurid curiosity."

"But that's not true," the FBI man said, "at least not in Barrett's case."

"That doesn't matter," the old man said. "She doesn't have to prove it, she just has to splash it all across the media. And there's just enough evidence to make it believable to the masses."

"Will she betray her own family for a promotion?" the senator asked, sounding doubtful.

"She will. We've just found evidence that she's been cheating on her rancher husband for years. She's got a lover in Phoenix. Her production editor, as a matter of fact. She doesn't give a damn about the Chase family."

"Perfect!" the FBI man crowed. "Send over that information and I'll get right to work on it, sir."

"I will." The old man's voice sounded faint, as if the effort of saying a few sentences was almost too much for him. But his voice, while weak, carried a note of strength.

The strength that comes from knowing one was about to emerge triumphant.

NOW AVAILABLE!

<u>THE KILLING PLACE</u>
(An Alexa Chase Suspense Thriller—Book 6)

When a witness in a witness protection program is killed, U.S. Marshal Alexa Chase assumes it's related to the case. But when she hits dead ends and the mystery becomes far more complex, she realizes a serial killer may be at work. What is his pattern? Can she connect the dots in time?

"This is an excellent book… When you start reading, be sure you don't have to wake up early!"
—Reader review for The Killing Game

The Killing Place (An Alexa Chase Suspense Thriller—Book 6) is book #6 in a new series by mystery and suspense author Kate Bold, which begins with THE KILLING GAME (Book #1).

Alexa Chase, 34, a brilliant profiler in the FBI's Behavioral Analysis Unit, was too good at her job. Haunted by all the serial killers she caught, she left a stunning career behind to join the U.S. Marshals. As a Deputy Marshal, Alexa—fit, and as tough as she is brilliant—could immerse herself in a simple career of hunting down fugitives and bringing them to justice.

But with her recent work a big success, the FBI and the Marshals have decided to make their joint-task force permanent. Alexa, reeling from her own traumatic past and her PTSD of hunting serial killers, has no choice: she will now have to work with an FBI partner she dislikes and hunt down serial killers whose jurisdiction intertwines with that of the U.S. Marshals. Alexa finds herself forced to confront the thing she dreads the most—entering a killer's mind.

As Alexa dives deeper into the investigation, she realizes suspects are everywhere—and the clock is ticking. But who can really be trusted?

All Alexa can do is rely on her brilliant skills to enter the killer's twisted mind before he strikes again.

A page-turning and harrowing crime thriller featuring a brilliant and tortured Deputy Marshal, the ALEXA CHASE series is a riveting mystery, packed with non-stop action, suspense, twists and turns, revelations, and driven by a breakneck pace that will keep you flipping pages late into the night.

Future books in the series will be available soon.

"This book moved very fast and every page was exciting. Plenty of dialogue, you absolutely love the characters, and you were rooting for the good guy throughout the whole story… I look forward to reading the next in the series."
—Reader review for The Killing Game

"Kate did an amazing job on this book and I was hooked from the first chapter!"
—Reader review for The Killing Game

"I really enjoyed this book. The characters were authentic, and I see the bad guys as something we hear about daily on the news... Looking forward to book 2."
—Reader review for The Killing Game

"This was a really good book. The main characters were real, flawed and human. The story went along quickly and wasn't mired in too many unnecessary details. I really enjoyed it."
—Reader review for The Killing Game

"Alexa Chase is headstrong, impatient, but most of all brave with a capital B. She never, repeat never, backs down until the bad guys are put where they belong. Clearly five stars!"
—Reader review for The Killing Game

“Captivating and riveting serial murder with a twist of the macabre… Very well done.”
—Reader review for The Killing Game

“WOW what a great read! Talk about a diabolical killer! Really enjoyed this book. Looking forward to reading others by this author as well.”
—Reader review for The Killing Game

“Page turner for sure. Great characters and relationships. I got into the middle of this story and couldn’t put it down. Looking forward to more from Kate Bold.”
—Reader review for The Killing Game

“Hard to put down. It has an excellent plot and has the right amount of suspense. I really enjoyed this book.”
—Reader review for The Killing Game

“Extremely well written, and well worth buying and reading. I can't wait to read book two!”
—Reader review for The Killing Game

Kate Bold

Bestselling author Kate Bold is author of the ALEXA CHASE SUSPENSE THRILLER series, comprising six books (and counting); the ASHLEY HOPE SUSPENSE THRILLER series, comprising six books (and counting); the CAMILLE GRACE FBI SUSPENSE THRILLER series, comprising five books (and counting); and the HARLEY COLE FBI SUSPENSE THRILLER series, comprising three books (and counting).

An avid reader and lifelong fan of the mystery and thriller genres, Kate loves to hear from you, so please feel free to visit www.kateboldauthor.com to learn more and stay in touch.

BOOKS BY KATE BOLD

ALEXA CHASE SUSPENSE THRILLER
THE KILLING GAME (Book #1)
THE KILLING TIDE (Book #2)
THE KILLING HOUR (Book #3)
THE KILLING POINT (Book #4)
THE KILLING FOG (Book #5)
THE KILLING PLACE (Book #6)

ASHLEY HOPE SUSPENSE THRILLER
LET ME GO (Book #1)
LET ME OUT (Book #2)
LET ME LIVE (Book #3)
LET ME BREATHE (Book #4)
LET ME FORGET (Book #5)
LET ME ESCAPE (Book #6)

CAMILLE GRACE FBI SUSPENSE THRILLER
NOT ME (Book #1)
NOT NOW (Book #2)
NOT WELL (Book #3)
NOT HER (Book #4)
NOT NORMAL (Book #5)

HARLEY COLE FBI SUSPENSE THRILLER
NOWHERE SAFE (Book #1)
NOWHERE LEFT (Book #2)
NOWHERE TO RUN (Book #3)

www.ingramcontent.com/pod-product-compliance
Lightning Source LLC
Chambersburg PA
CBHW030617310726
48979CB00003B/752

9781094395449